A Journey Out of Season

Mary Hansen

Desiana Publications
Bellingham Washington

Published by Desiana Publication
Copyright © Mary Hansen 2019
Desiana Publications Bellingham, Washington.

ISBN: 978-0-578-58588-8

Cover design by Toby Mikle
Interior images: Toby Mikle, Credit to Washington Historical
Museum for picture of Chief Joseph Family (public domain).

Desiana Publications
1510 N. Forest #413
Bellingham, Washington 98225
desianabooks@outlook.com

This is a work of historical fiction. Exact events in the work
are the product of the authors imagination. The names of
geographical featured and historical events that do not coincide
with the story narrative are generally historically accurate.

Acknowledgements:

I wish to express my gratitude to my editor Virginia Herrick for her many hours of patient work and valuable advice.

I would like to thank the young readers who reviewed this work and offered their suggestions, especially the third-grade students at San Francisco Friends School.

Also, I am appreciative for the support of Friends from Bellingham Friends Meeting and University Friends Meeting for holding me in the Light through the many months of work that have passed during this project.

Finally, the support of Washington State Division of Services for the Blind has been helpful in bringing this book to print.

This Book is Dedicated

To the generations of Quakers.
Especially The WWII war resisters and those
youth who keep us conscientious now.

TABLE OF CONTENTS

GRANDPA RUFUS

When my sister and I and our cousins visited the big house on Garden Street in Bellingham, Washington, we'd often find Grandpa Rufus sitting by the fireplace. Today, he was!

He looked up from his reading as we came in. His eyes were bright and friendly, and the wrinkles on his face curved around his smile when he saw us.

It was a rainy, cold day, and we wanted a story about the trip he had taken when he was a little boy, from Iowa to Washington with his grandma and his dog, Barclay. That was way back, near the end of the Second World War. We liked Grandpa Rufus's stories.

"Grandpa, tell us about Thomas B!" we said. We knew the story of his trip was the very first Thomas Bear story.

He stood up and took the old bear down from his chair on the mantle. We all got comfortable.

By the time we met him, Thomas had two felt eyes of a kind of blue-black color, a black, wrinkled nose, and a squiggly-looking smile. His nose was turned to one side of his face, which made him look like he was kind of unsure of things. One of his overall straps was held up with a gold safety pin. The look on his face was one of eternal questioning. We loved him.

Grandpa Rufus got Thomas B (the "B" was for Bear) because his parents had to go back to Europe and couldn't be with him for a while when he was a little boy.

My sister and I were Thomases, just like Grandpa Rufus. He was our dad's father. Our cousins had other last names, because they were the kids of my dad's sisters. He had three sisters and no brothers.

This time, all of us cousins had come for a sleepover so we could get Grandpa to tell stories for hours. That was the most fun we could imagine on a long, wet weekend.

Grandpa Rufus looked at us, his face lit up with that warm smile that was almost a laugh. His eyes were bright with mischief.

"One thing I always have to remind you of before we start one of my stories," he said. "Way back then, when I was a boy, things were just a little different."

"A little!" I exclaimed, because I knew what he was going to say. Then he did laugh.

"Well, we did have two legs and arms and we did speak English. But we did not talk to our friends on Facebook, or even watch TV. We could not just call up anytime we wanted. A lot of people still didn't even have telephones. There were no cell phones. If you were traveling you might find a pay phone if you were lucky, but it was very expensive to call anywhere except your own town. And calling another country was almost impossible. In emergencies people sent something called telegrams. Mostly people sent letters to get in touch with others who were far away, and letters took a few days or a few weeks to arrive. So when my parents were away, we didn't hear from them for weeks. We could call people in the same country, but only when we were at the right place and at certain times, and they had to be home when you called. Sometimes we listened to the radio, but that was a special occasion and the weather had to be good. And believe it or not, there were no computers.

"But there is one other important thing I have to tell you that I forgot the first time I told this story. What has changed even more

since I was a boy, is how people think and talk about things. Back in 1945, we called Native Americans "Indians." We called African Americans "negros," or "colored people." Now we know better. Now we try to call people first by their names, but if they are part of a group we need to name, we use the terms that they want us to use. Many Native American people like to be identified with the nation that they belong to, like Sioux or Nez Perce. European Americans back then, even the ones who were Quakers, had a lot to learn.

"Well, the Thomas B story I am going to tell today has to start with someone else . . ."

IOWA

*T*he story really begins before I got Thomas B, you know. The story begins back in Iowa, in the winter, before the war ended.

Mum, Dad, Grandpa, Grandma, and I were all home, listening to the radio. It was almost my bedtime when we heard a very loud racket coming from the chicken house. Grandpa grabbed a pellet gun. It was not for killing whatever was attacking the chickens, although he might use it to scare the thief away. Sadly, it was to shoot any hen who might be so badly injured that she could not be saved.

Grandpa went out first, and we all followed at a safe distance.

"Get out of my hen house!" Grandpa shouted.

Out came a scruffy, black-and-white dog. He was dirty and scratched from crawling under the barbed wire fence. He was so thin that we could see his ribs. As soon as he saw us, he fell on his stomach and covered his nose with his paws.

"I think he might be apologizing," said Mum.

"We should call him Barclay," Grandpa said with a laugh. I didn't know it then, but that was a joke about a famous Quaker who wrote an essay called "Barclay's Apology."

My dad thought that was pretty funny.

"Are the chickens all right?" I asked.

"I'll go see," Grandpa said.

"I'll get the slop pail," Grandma said. "Poor thing must be starving." The slop pail was where we kept the scraps from our meals, to feed to the pig.

"Why don't you set it down over by the fence?" Dad suggested. "He'll probably eat once we've gone in."

Grandma walked toward the fence and Barclay got up from his "apology" and followed her. As soon as she set the bucket down, he started eating. She stood there, looking at him for a moment, and then she bent down and stroked his long back. His tail began to wag.

Grandpa came back from inspecting the chickens and said, "All the hens are okay. They sure are mad, though."

Grandpa put an old blanket on the screened porch that night and left the door propped open. When he went out to milk the next morning, that's where he found Barclay sleeping. Grandpa put some medicine he used on the cows on Barclay's scratches, and after a few days we let him sleep in the house. He especially loved Grandma. I think maybe it was her cooking, or her kindness.

⚘

My mum and dad had met just as the war was starting to get bad in Europe. They were in London, England. People were afraid that England was going to be bombed by the Germans. My mum was a nurse with the British Red Cross. Grandpa and Dad were with the Friends Ambulance Service.

The German army had taken over some of the countries in Europe that were just across the water from England. Families were starting to send their children to the countryside, and even to Canada and the United States, to keep them safer if the big cities were bombed. My dad and grandpa wanted to keep people safe, and they hoped that they could help stop the war.

My dad and mum met each other over there when all this was going on. Anyway, they got married in England.

Because my mum was about to have me and all the children were moving to safer places, my grandpa insisted that they come back to Iowa, where he and Grandma and Dad were from. This was before the United States was even part of World War II, so it was much safer here.

Well, the safest way to get back was on a ship, although ships got sunk by the Germans sometimes. But that didn't happen to their ship. What did happen was that I couldn't wait to be born: I was born on that ship, in the middle of the Atlantic Ocean! It was in early December 1939. So my grandparents would tease me and tell me I was a citizen of the Great Atlantic.

༄

Almost a year after I was born, the planes started bombing London. Mum got worried about all her people who were still there: her mum and dad and her sister, and all the people who lived in London who had no safe place to go. Dad and Grandpa felt they should go there and help too. I stayed with Grandma, and they went back to London during the Blitz. That's what they called the German bombing of the English cities.

One night, Dad was helping some people get to an underground shelter when part of a building fell on him and broke his leg. So Grandpa sent him home again to rest and to be safe.

When he got to Iowa, my dad's leg was a lot worse. It hadn't been set right, and he had to have surgery. He had a limp for the rest of his life. Because he was a Quaker and a conscientious objector, he was not allowed by the government to go back overseas during the war. Because of his leg and the farm, they didn't try to make him go to war or do other service.

Grandpa came home soon after that. He did go back to England, and so did Mum, from time to time. But Dad stayed home all through the rest of the war.

Most of what I remember from when I was little was the farm and the neighbors. We had some older men and young women helping us with the cows and the corn. Almost all the young men had gone to war. I guess it was a big farm, for those days. Dad did what he could. He did a lot of writing and studying at the college in Ames. Grandma was always busy cooking and helping the neighbors, and I was helping her, going visiting with her, feeding the calves, and playing with the few children who lived nearby. It seemed like all the people we knew were Friends. This is how I thought the world was. The furthest I had been from home was into Ames a few times to go shopping, or to visit the college with Grandpa.

Some of the older Quaker folks still talked like Grandma with her "thees and "thys." Some, like Grandma, still wore Plain Dress: gray and white clothes, with bonnets for women and flat-brimmed hats for men.

There was always a lot to do when we lived on the farm. I had to help, mostly getting things for people. If Grandpa needed a tool and Dad was in the shed, he would ask me to go have Dad find it and send it back with me. And every day when the mail truck driver put letters in our box, I would bring them in to Grandma.

Grandma got a lot of letters. She had friends in lots of different places. It seems like they would write to her about some important things, and she would think about it a lot, talk to Grandpa, and then write back to them. I learned later that Grandma was a law-yer, except, because she wasn't a man, she didn't get to be a "real" one back then. Things are different now. I guess there was no law about it. Most people were just very unfriendly to women lawyers.

During the war, there weren't enough teachers, so the schools were very crowded and sometimes kids had to go to school in shifts: early in the morning, or later in the day, so they could use the school building and teachers two times a day and teach more kids.

My parents and some other people didn't want their kids to go there. When I was supposed to start school, I went to Emma Moss's living room three afternoons a week, with some other children, and learned to read, write, and do simple arithmetic. At first, she used some books she had about the letters of the alphabet. Soon, however, she had us dictating to her and then reading the stories about things we did and liked. The stories were about how we felt and what was happening in our lives.

She would use examples from around the farm to help with learning numbers and adding and subtracting. Emma Moss was a retired teacher, so everyone said that was just great. Actually, I think it gave some of us a head start.

I don't really remember when the war ended. I do remember Grandpa saying one day, "Well, now that the war is over and all the fighting has stopped, things will have to be rebuilt in Europe. There are very few schools left after all the fighting and bombing. Many buildings and homes have been destroyed. There are people just wandering in the streets. Children are left on their own with nowhere to go. Their parents are dead, missing, or just busy trying to find food to feed them. They need schools, or they, too, will be lost."

My mum knew that many people were sick and injured after the war and there were no clinics and hospitals to take care of them. They needed medical help. They needed nurses.

So very soon after the war ended, Mum, Dad, and Grandpa had to go back over to Europe to help. It was something they all felt they had to do, because they knew how and it was the right thing to do.

Before they left, Mum and Dad got Thomas B to keep me company. Then, when he was new, he was a little fatter and a brighter brown. He had two black button eyes, a button nose, and a big red felt smile. We made him a yarn smile when that first one fell off. Mum made him a pair of blue overalls, just like mine. Dad made him that chair and painted it glossy red.

Thomas B became a great friend of mine! I would tell him things that I had always told Mum when she was home. I knew he was listening, because he would have that look on his face, with his head turned to one side. Sometimes I thought he would say "uh-huh" in the certain special way Mum used to always say it. A way that told me she'd heard. Not like Grandma, who sometimes said, "I see," but I could tell she really didn't.

Especially when Mum and Dad were away, I tried to tell Thomas B everything important so I wouldn't forget any of it. But there did come a time when even Thomas B wasn't there—a time when I had to remember by myself.

❧

It was almost winter when Grandpa and my parents had to leave on the train. I was very sad. I cried because I didn't want them to go. I couldn't go with them, and I didn't want to stay just with my Grandma Elizabeth. I loved my grandmother, but it was lonely, just the two of us. And she didn't know how to have fun very much. And they weren't even going to be home for my birthday.

Grandma said they would be gone only a few months—half a year. When I was a boy, arguing with grown-ups was not something children did. So, I just nodded and said, "Okay." But I knew half a year was a very long time.

Grandma kept a schedule. That meant that everything was done at a certain time, the same time, the same way, every day. Certain things were done on certain days of the week: washing on Monday; ironing on Wednesday; shopping on Saturday. I even had to play on schedule.

It seemed not very long at all after the train had left—only a few days really—that Grandma sat down with me at the plank table. She filled her teacup and smiled down on me.

Grandma was often serious, and when she smiled a certain way, it was usually to make me understand something. Her smile meant that I should know that what she was telling me was for my own good and that it would make me a happier person when I understood it. Like why it was important to be silent in Meeting and kind and helpful with older people and little children. I really didn't mind these things, and it was nice to see Grandma smile.

"Rufus," she said, making me feel like a grown-up, "thee knows that we are here and the rest of the family is doing some very important work, helping people overseas?"

I nodded.

"Well, I got a letter from thy grandfather, and he has been offered a job way out in Washington State. So it is up to thee and me to get the family moved out there before they all get back from Europe."

In my young mind one did not move people, one moved things or livestock. *"We need to help the Bruces move the sheep to uphill pastures."* Or, *"Emma Moss needs help moving the piano."* Pictures of handcarts and barking collies floated through my head.

"You mean we are moving the house out there. We don't move people. We move things," I said.

I think we both realized the most amazing thing at the same time. I did not understand her world completely, and she did not understand mine. We sat looking at each other for a while.

She sat her teacup down on the plank table. "I'm going to explain how it works, this moving thing." And she did, from start to finish. She answered all my questions. It was one of the nicest things anyone had ever done for me.

Over the next few days, neighbor women and women from our Meeting came to our house. They put dishes and pans, sheets and table linens, blankets and towels, and finally even the pictures from the walls into boxes. They talked and laughed and cried. They brought food and pies and cookies for me. They even made me mittens and hats. They said it was not the season for moving. Winter was a hard time to move. They all said they would miss me and Grandma. All this caused me to have more questions for my grandmother. I had no idea how far away we were going.

So we sat down again at the plank table, and Grandma told me about the trip. This time I didn't have questions right away; I was too amazed. We were going to go in the car. We were going to drive to the city and then keep going, for days and days.

I felt scared.

"Is Thomas Bear coming with us in the car?"

"Of course he is," Grandma reassured me.

⚘

I went to bed with Thomas tucked under my arm that Saturday. The next afternoon the moving truck would come to take our boxes. What I didn't understand was that the movers would also take all the furniture.

The next morning, I heard Grandma moving around downstairs. It was already a bright morning, so I hurriedly got into my clothes and ready for Meeting.

It was a quiet Meeting. Only one woman spoke. At the rise of Meeting, Grandma said a few words about how important the Meeting had been in the life of our family. After that, everyone came over to talk with us and say goodbye. Then we went to the Bruces' house to eat dinner.

When we got back to the house, the biggest truck I had ever seen was parked between the barn and the house. I had to stop and lean against the pump handle. That truck was so big I almost fell over, looking up at it. The running board on that truck was as high as my head. Standing beside it were a small woman and a man who looked a bit like Grandpa.

"We been waitin' fer ya to sign the papers. Got everything loaded," said the man. "Shut yer dog in the barn. Didn't want her ta git hurt or run off."

Grandma put her hand out. "Elizabeth Thomas," she said.

"Oh, yeah, I'm Harvey Hatter, an' this is my wife, Betty," said the man.

I worked my way around the big truck and over to the porch to look at all the things Grandma had put out to be packed in the car. Where was Thomas Bear?

I ran through the open screen door, up the stairs, and straight into my room. It was totally empty, no furniture; just the floor and the walls. Something was terribly wrong!

The next thing I heard was Grandma's voice above me.

"Rufus, what happened?" She wiped my forehead with a damp handkerchief.

I looked up at her. "Where's Thomas? Where's my . . . ? Grandma?!"

She carried me downstairs and laid me on the back seat of the car. She made a cold compress from a towel she found in the milking parlor and put it on my forehead.

"Just rest," she said. "When we get to town, I will call the moving company about thy bear. I think they just packed him with thy bedding. We haven't lost him."

"What happened?" I asked, not sure what I meant.

"I think thee fainted," said Grandma. "Just rest."

So now it was just me and Grandma—and Barclay. Pretty soon Barclay and everything we'd packed for the trip was in the car. Barclay licked my face and then settled down on the floor.

We bumped along, all the way to Ames on gravel roads. Grandma pulled over where I could see the gas station's flying-horse sign from where I was lying. She got out of the car with her coin purse and said, "I will make a few calls and be right back."

❦

"The moving company people will ask the Hatters about thy bear when they call in first thing in the morning," she said when she got back in the car.

"We will be at the Nelsons' in about four hours. Thee remembers Emily and Sarah from Yearly Meeting, doesn't thee? We will spend a few days with them before we head on into South Dakota."

Oh, I remembered Sarah and Emily all right! They had wrapped me in a blanket and tried to feed me with a baby bottle. I guess they thought I was the little brother they wished they had. I groaned.

"Is thee all right, Rufus?" Grandma asked.

"Tired," I said.

MENDING FENCES

When I woke, Barclay was on top of me, it was dark, and
we had stopped.

"Wake up," said Grandma. "We're here."

I pushed the dog off, and he bounded out the open door.

Emily and Sarah Nelson's house was really little. There were
two little windows in front with a door in the middle. I saw
Emily's face peeking out from the window where she had pulled
the curtain aside.

By the time I sat up, her mother was in the open doorway,
hugging Grandma. I grabbed my pillow, got out of the car, and
followed Grandma up onto the porch.

Emily squeezed by her mother, Margaret.

"Rufus!" she squealed, running at me.

"I'm not a baby!" I yelled, without thinking.

Grandma turned and stared at me, her mouth open.

"Rufus! Don't you remember, your dad explained that to us?
That was a long time ago," Emily pleaded.

She did look a little more grown-up too.

"I'm sorry," I said. "I just woke up."

"Come on in," said Margaret Nelson.

"Stay!" said Grandma to Barclay.

"He better come in too," said Margaret Nelson. "We've had bears here lately. What's his name?"

"Barclay," I said.

Barclay came in, and a big yellow cat hissed at him. He immediately fell on his stomach and put his paws over his nose.

"That's his apology," I said.

"'Barclay's Apology,'" said Emily's mother and started to laugh, just like my dad. "So that's why you call him Barclay. Don't worry, boy; that cat won't hurt you. She is just noisy."

We had some dinner, and then Sarah and Emily's mom showed us where we would sleep. They had a sleeping loft, which was kind of an attic that you had to get to by climbing a ladder. Everyone slept up there. There were two small beds and one large one. The girls and I were going to sleep in the big one. It had a feather bed on top. The girls were to sleep on one end and I on the other with our feet in the middle with a quilt over us. Grandma would sleep in one of the little beds on one side and Margaret Nelson on the other side.

Before we went to bed, we all went out to the outhouse. They didn't have any indoor plumbing. I was looking around for that bear and listening for all the night sounds. Barclay smelled everywhere, and Grandma was being really strict with him.

Even the adults went right to bed and turned out the gas light. I guess it was pretty late. I lay there in the dark, feeling all alone, at the end of the feather bed under that big quilt. It was so soft and so deep that I couldn't see anyone or anything. I started to cry.

Sarah must have heard me. "What's the trouble, Rufus?"

"I miss my bear, I miss my Mum, and I miss my Daddy," I sobbed.

Grandma got up and sat on the bed and gave me a hug. Emily put a big floppy doll on the bed next to me. "You can sleep with Raggedy Andy. I miss my Daddy too. He's in jail."

"Let's hold all of our loved ones in the Light, and each other as well," said Margaret Nelson.

"And our bears, too," I added.

There was a little silence, and then Grandma said, "I think that we will find that Thomas the Bear is safe with the Hatters on the moving truck."

After that, I fell asleep.

⁂

When I woke, a spot of sun was on the quilt near Raggedy Andy and me. He had orange yarn hair and was staring up at me from the feather bed. I heard Grandma and Margaret Nelson talking downstairs and could smell coffee and oatmeal. I crawled to the edge of the bed and rolled off onto the floor with a thud. It was the only way I could think of to get out of the big bed.

"Rufus!" Grandma called. "Is thee all right?"

"I'm all right," I said. Apparently, Sarah and Emily had already gone downstairs. I climbed back down the ladder and, sure enough, there they were at the table, looking sleepy.

"Have some oatmeal?" asked Margaret Nelson.

"Rufus, put on thy trousers!" exclaimed Grandma. I was standing there in my long underwear. Only Grandma seemed to notice or care.

After we all ate, drank coffee, and cleaned up, Grandma called the company that the Hatters drove for. The woman she talked to said that the Hatters would be calling in around noon and she would ask them about my bear then. They arranged to call back at the Nelsons' the next morning.

"How long are we going to stay?" I asked. I thought the sooner we got to Washington, the sooner I would see Thomas B and Mum and Dad.

"We will stay a few days, Rufus. We will help the Nelsons with their farm, and some Friends are coming by to help too," Grandma said.

"Okay," I said.

"Today we will help mend some fences. So thee and I will go to town for some supplies."

⚛

On the way into town I had a chance to ask Grandma the question that had been in my mind. "Grandma, why did Emily and Sarah's dad go to jail?"

"Quakers don't believe in fighting in wars or killing other people," she said. "Jack Nelson refused to join the army, so they arrested him and sent him to prison."

"Grandpa and Daddy don't fight, but they aren't in jail," I said.

She smiled that smile and said, "Well, Jack wasn't in the Friends Ambulance Service like they were when the war started. He didn't sign up to do alternative service. He didn't believe he should have anything at all to do with war. But also—and this is the hard part—thee knows that the Nelsons are poor, and Jack wanted to stay and take care of his family. He didn't know how they would make it without him. So he waited as long as he could, and he hoped that the government would just forget about him.

"When there was trouble in England, Grandpa and your dad went over there to help the people who were being hurt and to see how they could help to stop the war. They could afford to do that because our family has some extra money and we could afford to hire people to help out on the farm. After thee was born, we didn't have to worry about making enough money or having food to feed thee. I was here to take care of thee, and we had plenty of money and food. But it has been really hard for Margaret and the girls without Jack here to work on the farm."

That was the first time I had ever thought about anyone maybe not having enough of what they needed. I mean, Mum talked about children in Europe not having enough. That didn't seem real; it was more like a story to me. But this was someone I knew.

"Well, eventually, when he didn't sign up to go to war, they arrested him and sent him to prison for refusing to fight," Grandma added.

"I thought prison was only for bad people," I said. Grandma just gave me that smile again.

We went to the general store in the town near the Nelsons' farm, and we bought so much stuff that it filled the back seat and the trunk also. We bought not only nails and wire but also meat and vegetables and a pair of gloves for me and also a collar and rope for Barclay.

Back at the farm, I got out of the car, and I could hear Barclay barking and whining loudly from inside the house. I ran in and found that he was upstairs, looking down from loft.

"How did he get up there?" I asked. Barclay was peeking over the edge of the loft.

"Barclay! No, Barclay, no!" shouted Grandma. "Stay!"

"Stay right here, Rufus! Don't let him jump or he will hurt himself," Grandma told me, as she rushed out the door.

I climbed the ladder and held Barclay as he whimpered and licked me.

Soon Margaret Nelson came in, dragging her oldest daughter behind her.

"He wanted to go up, so we helped him," Sarah pleaded with her mother.

"Well, you better figure out how he's going to get down, and soon. He has to go," Margaret Nelson warned. She was mad.

They couldn't carry him down; he was too big. Sarah finally wrapped him in an old sheet and lowered him down, but he was so frightened that he wet the sheet.

Margaret made the girls rinse the sheet out at the pump in the yard and hang it to dry. That was a pretty cold job. The girls promised that next time they would think before they did something like that.

Barclay was pretty embarrassed and kept apologizing for the rest of the day.

By this time, people were starting to arrive, mostly women. Grandma handed me my work gloves and told me my job was to find all of the places that needed fixing along the fence. She gave me a handful of little flags on sticks and walked along with me slowly until we found a few places that needed mending or had loose poles that need replacing. When we found one, we would place a flag in the ground near it. Then she explained that when people finished fixing things, they would bring me their flags so that I could mark new places.

"When thee comes to the corner, just turn it and keep right on going," said Grandma. Then she left me to my job.

Before long people were bringing me flags. I felt good about this job. I got to the end of that side of the fence and turned the corner. It was starting to snow. After a while, I began to feel cold and tired and hungry. It had been a long time since Grandma had left me. I couldn't see the house. Where was Grandma? It must be getting very late. I didn't know if I could go on. It seemed like it took forever for someone to bring me a new flag. Then I told the woman to find my grandma. I needed to talk to her.

"It must be getting very late. I'm really tired," I said to Grandma when she showed up. Then I noticed she was wearing Grandpa's overalls, which were covered with mud. Her pant legs were soaked up to the knee, and she looked pretty tired too.

"We have to finish mending the fences; then we'll be able to eat the lunch that Cora is making for us. Come on, Rufus. I'll give thee a hand," Grandma replied.

That made me feel better. I remembered Cora from Yearly Meeting. She loved to cook and made some of the best food we had to eat. She was older than my grandma and a little rounder. Cooking seemed to be her special gift.

Grandma didn't really do my work. She just followed along with me and encouraged me. When we came to the rise of the hill, I could see the farmhouse ahead, and the end of the row where the barbed wire fencing ended. The chicken wire that was connected to the chicken shed and the other end of the farmyard was all that was left.

"We're done," I said.

"We'll have to go to the barn and scrape off all this mud before we can go into the house," said Grandma.

I looked around and noticed that people were making repairs on the roofs of the house and the barn. There were a lot more cars parked in the yard, and people were still turning in flags to me.

In the barn we took a hoe and scraped a lot of mud off our overalls and swept a lot of water and mud from our clothes. I turned my boots over and poured water from them. Grandma gave me a dry pair of socks and we both put our boots on and walked back to the house.

"We'll have to wait until everyone is finished before we can eat," she said.

Cora was stirring a big pot of something on the stove, and there were fresh-baked rolls on the table. I looked in the pot and saw the vegetables and meat that we had bought in the store. Soon more and more people were coming into the house.

Cora smiled at me and put a hand on my shoulder. "It's time to call the workers from the roof. It's time to eat," she said.

After a silent grace, we all ate the stew. I listened carefully to the talk among the adults. I was interested to see whether others were like Emily and Sarah's father, or like my parents. It seemed like some other grown-ups were in jail too. And some other parents were overseas as well. The grown-ups had a lot of worries about what was happening in the world, and about their loved ones coming home safe. I think this was the first time I'd ever thought about that kind of thing.

After quite a while, some people got up and started to go back to work. Other families said their goodbyes to Margaret Nelson and the girls because they had a long way to drive. After most of the adults had gone outside, Margaret called the children to meet her by the fireplace.

"It's been a long day, and you children have worked hard. Now that it is almost dark, I think we will take some time to relax and play some games. But first I would like to tell you about something that happened to Barclay this morning. Rufus, could you call Barclay for us? I think he might like to take part in this," she said.

I wasn't so sure Barclay wanted to be a part of anything just then. I called to him, and there was a great clatter and banging from the pots and bins behind the stove. Barclay stuck his head out and looked at us. Seeing the girls and the other children, he whimpered and lay back down.

Then Cora pulled a big flat bone from the kettle on the stove and said, "Barclay, would you like a nice soup bone?" Barclay started to wag his tail and came right to her. The bone still had a lot of meat on it, and Cora placed it on a pie plate on the floor. Barclay, still wagging his tail, started to eat the delicious meat off the bone.

Margaret Nelson said, "I'm sure that right there will do just fine."

Then she put an arm around Sarah and said, "Sarah would you tell us what happened with Barclay this morning?"

"Well," said Sarah, looking down at her feet, "well, you see, um, Rufus and his grandma had to go to town, and Emily and I were doing the dishes and well, Barclay, I guess, he thought that Rufus was still upstairs because he went to the ladder and he put his paws up on the second rung and started whimpering.

"So Emily and I thought he wanted to go up there and look for Rufus. So we thought we should help him. So I got behind him, and I kind of pushed him and helped with his paws and, well, we kind of got him up there in the loft. It was kind of hard to get him up there; he is sort of heavy, and he doesn't really know how to climb a ladder. But when he got up there, he smelled all around and he looked for Rufus. He looked in the bed and he looked under the bed and he looked at Grandma's bed. Well, he looked pretty happy, and he lay down under the bed and sort of took a nap. So we left him right there and went out to do our chores in the barn," she said with a sigh.

"Okay," said Margaret Nelson. "Let's stop right here and see if anyone can see a problem. Well, anyone, except Rufus and Emily and Sarah. Take a look at Barclay. Now think about how you climb a ladder. Do you use your arms, your legs, or both? And what do you do when you come down the ladder? Now, if you were Barclay, how would you get down the ladder?"

A girl whose name was Alice said, "I would be pretty scared if I had paws instead of hands and more paws instead of feet. And besides that, before I knew how to come down the ladder, I was scared because I didn't know you had to go backward."

"Okay, Rufus," said Margaret Nelson, "can you tell us what happened when you got home from the store?"

"When I got out of the car," I replied," I heard Barclay whining and barking. When I came into the house, I saw him looking down from the loft and whining some more. Grandma was afraid he was going to jump and hurt himself. I think he was really scared."

"How did you get him down?" asked a boy named Riley.

"We had to wrap him in a sheet and lower him down," said Sarah. "But he was so scared he wet the sheet."

"And besides," said Emily, "we got in a lot of trouble."

"So what do you think the lesson is from this?" asked Margaret Nelson.

"Think before you do something stupid?" said Emily.

"What I want you to remember," said Margaret, "is to do a special kind of thinking."

"What do you mean?" I asked.

"I mean," said Margaret Nelson, "you should try to think about how the other person feels and thinks before you make decisions for them. You have to remember how they have to do things that are different from the way you do things. It's like if you go out the door and close it but forget that your little brother can't reach the doorknob."

"I get it," said Riley.

I got it too, mostly. I felt sorry for Barclay. I bet he felt like a trick had been played on him. I understood that Sarah and Emily did not mean to play a trick on him. Still . . . I was beginning to wonder if Sarah and Emily had a knack for getting in trouble.

In the years since then, I have also wondered if it was fair to use the girls to teach this lesson. It seems like they were feeling bad enough as it was. But back then, parents were pretty tough on us. I guess we made it through, mostly.

⚜

The rest of the evening, we played some games and sang some songs, and soon it was dark and time for a light supper and bed. I asked if I could stay downstairs and sleep with Barclay. There were several extra guests who had brought sleeping bags. Alice said that I could borrow her sleeping bag if she could sleep in the feather bed with Sarah and Emily. And I thought, *good luck*. I hoped she didn't get lost like I did.

Barclay curled up on the floor by the fireplace, right next to me. We both must have been really tired, because the thing that woke us up was the phone ringing the next morning.

Grandma was already up and dressed when she answered it. Some people were already out in the barn, working.

I sat up and listened. Barclay groaned and tried to turn over.

"Oh, good," said Grandma into the receiver. "He'll be happy to hear that! It's very important, you know . . .

"It sounds like they have children as well . . . Okay . . . Oh, the second? Next Monday? . . . Oh, my. Well, we are still in western Iowa . . . Well, we had best be on our way, then. I thank thee for helping with this. Yes, I will check with thee in a few days. Goodbye."

Right after hanging up, she turned to me. "Thy bear is safe, Rufus; he is riding in the cab with the Hatters.

"They will be delivering our things in less than a week," she went on, "so we will have to leave right away. We have to find my friend in South Dakota, and Montana is a very big state to cross.

"I must go talk with Margaret Nelson," Grandma went on as she headed out the door to the barn.

I had to find all my things, and Barclay's, and say a proper goodbye to the girls. Grandma had a lot of people to talk to before we could leave, but she did seem in a hurry all the same. There was quite a bit of snow on the ground, although it was no longer snowing.

SUNSHINE

*I*t was noon before we left with extra food packed for us by Cora. Barclay was curled up in the back, and I was sitting in front with Grandma. It had started to snow steadily now.

"I don't know if we will get to Pierre, South Dakota, today," said Grandma. "We may have to stay in a hotel tonight," she added after we were out on the road.

"A what?" I asked. I had never heard of a hotel. I had never stayed in anything but a house or a tent.

Now, most of Iowa is pretty flat. But as we passed east of the town of Ida Grove, I noticed we were going up hills and around more bends. I looked ahead, and through the snow I thought I saw mountains.

"Grandma," I said, "talking to Raggedy Andy was just not the same as talking to Thomas B. He has this real silly look on his face, and I think he is laughing at me. I don't think he understands how I feel."

Grandma looked surprised and maybe a little worried. "Thee talks to thy bear?" she asked.

"At night, just like I used to talk to Dad or Mum at bedtime. I miss them. And now I miss Thomas," I said.

"What does thee talk about?" she asked.

"I talk about what scares me," I answered, "and how I miss my parents or how I worry about things. And sometimes I tell him secrets that I don't want to tell anyone else."

"Oh," said Grandma with a sigh. "I see. Does thee ever ask him questions?"

"No," I said, "because I know he can't answer."

Then Grandma said something that really surprised me. "I miss my parents sometimes too, Rufus."

"You have parents?" I said.

Grandma laughed. "Well, they died quite a while ago, but I still miss them sometimes."

"Were they Quakers like you?" I asked. "Did they talk like you?" I wanted to know a lot.

"Well, of course, Rufus, they were Friends," Grandma said. "My father was a doctor. And when I was a girl, we traveled all over the West, taking health care to all kinds of people who had no doctor."

"Did they have to go to Europe during the war?" I asked.

"No, the war didn't happen back then," she said, smiling. "We had other kinds of troubles. It seems like people always have some kind of trouble," she added with a kind of faraway look.

For a while we didn't talk. It seemed like my grandmother was somewhere else in her mind. She was watching the road, but she was also thinking about something.

I was almost asleep; the bright sun against the snow and the sound of the wheels made me drowsy.

Finally, Grandma said, "It was on one of our trips in the north part of South Dakota that I met the friend of mine who we are going to see. My father was up there, helping a band of Sioux Indians with some medical issues.

"We were going through the hills with our wagon and I thought I heard singing of some kind, so I ran ahead, up a little incline to a clearing in the trees. An Indian boy, with his face painted, was dancing and singing a high-pitched, chanting kind of song. He was dancing really fast, and I thought he was about to fall right over the cliff.

"'Look out!' I yelled, as loud as I could. I raced over to pull him back just in time. The only thing was, I tripped over a tree root and fell down the slope myself. I heard something snap, and it wasn't the tree. It hurt terribly, and I yelled for my father.

"The boy started yelling at me, but I didn't understand him. He had a knife and I think he was threatening me, but I was in too much pain to even think about that. My mother and father came running up from the main road. My older brother took away the boy's knife. My father asked him what he did to me."

"Did you think he was going to kill you, Grandma?" I asked.

"I was just too scared to think, Rufus," she said. "He told my father that he was doing a very important dance, and that I had stopped it. He spoke English pretty well. After some back-and-forth, it became clear what had happened."

"Meanwhile, Mother came to me and found that I had a compound fracture. Which means that my leg bone was broken so badly that it was sticking out of the skin."

"It's a good thing," I said, "that your father was a doctor."

"My father and older brother carried me carefully back up into the clearing. My father had to set my leg and bandage it," Grandma continued.

"All the time this was going on, the young Sioux was angrily repeating that we should all be killed, that he hated soldiers and settlers after what that the soldiers had done to his family."

Finally, my mother said, "We're not soldiers or settlers, we're Quakers."

"He looked at her like this was some kind of trick, which it was, in a way. But in another way, it wasn't, because it meant that we wouldn't hurt or trick the Indians like others had. We always kept our word, as well as we understood it.

"Then she told him that I had saved his life and now he had to take care of me. (I think this was because she wanted him to stay with us for a while.)

"And then my mother asked the questions that she had been wondering about. 'Is thee Sioux?'

"'Yes, I am,' said the boy.

"'Is thee a girl?' my mother asked.

"'Yes! But I will be a warrior!' the girl, who we had thought was a boy, said. Then she told my mother how the soldiers had killed her parents and others, early one morning just a few months earlier, at a place called Wounded Knee, and how she had become determined to fight for her people."

(In December of 1890 the soldiers had come upon the encampment at Wounded Knee and, using the excuse that one brave still had a gun, had killed almost everyone in the camp. Sunshine and her sister had been out gathering wood and had escaped by hiding.)

"And the girl, who was not that much older than I, stopped, as if thinking something through carefully. 'I am a warrior and a woman. That is my right,' she said firmly. (My mother said later she didn't know if Sioux customs agreed with that.)"

"Was she really big and strong?" I asked.

"Not at all, Rufus," said Grandma, "but she tried really hard to make us think she was.

"'Goodness, thee certainly is "little Miss Sunshine,"' my father commented. So that became her nickname with our family. She really didn't like my father to tease her like that. But her name in Sioux was hard for me to pronounce. So I was the only one she allowed to call her Sunshine."

"My mother told me most of this afterward," Grandma added. "My pain was so great that I kept fainting. My father had to set my leg and bind it, because the bone was sticking out through the skin below my knee. He made me drink something that burned my throat. But I passed out again. When I woke, I was wedged among the supplies in the back of the wagon, and Sunshine was sitting on top of a box, looking down at me.

"'You're lucky,' she said to me. 'Your people usually shoot a horse when he breaks his leg.'"

I laughed.

"Does that mean she thought they should shoot you too?" I asked Grandma.

"No," Grandma said. "She was just teasing.

"Later," she went on, "we stopped at a village where my father had treated some people for food poisoning. After a few days, we were about to come to the place where Sunshine knew some of the Sioux people. She became upset and argued with my father, saying that she would not stay with us. It turns out that there was a mission school at that place. She said they wouldn't allow the children to wear Indian clothing and would not permit them to speak their language or practice their special dance. She was afraid if she went with us, the school leaders would take her away and make her go to school there.

"After a while, my father agreed to let us make camp outside of the village, and he went, by himself, in to treat the people there. When he came back, he said that many of the people seemed listless and subdued. He also said that he did not see many of the Sioux men there. Sunshine thought perhaps they were warriors who had been killed by the soldiers.

"After a few months, my father took the binding off my leg. When I was walking around, Sunshine told my mother that she would go back to her people as soon as she had finished her quest to become a warrior. My father asked her who she was going to make war against. She said she did not know because the spirit would have to show her the way. My mother wondered how she would avoid the school. She said that when she had finished her search, it would be clear that she was an adult, and no one could force her to go to school. Mother thought that this might be wishful thinking."

"Did they ever make her go to school?" I asked. "Did she have to stop dancing? What if she wanted to learn but still wanted to wear Indian clothes? That sounds mean."

"I suppose it was mean, Rufus," said Grandma. "European settlers tried to convince themselves that the Indians would be better off if they were just like us." She sighed.

"Sunshine, however," Grandma told me, "managed to get educated and keep herself just the way she wanted to be. Shortly after that, Sunshine left us to continue her quest.

"Over the next few years we lost track of Sunshine," Grandma continued. "Then one summer, when I was about sixteen, we stopped at the Standing Rock Reservation. Sunshine was living there as an honored member of the community.

"We found that she was married to an older medicine man and had two sons. She was, indeed, a formidable adult; I could see how no one could force her to do anything.

"She was glad to see us. She told us that she had learned that she could only fight with her voice and her strong back for now, but that someday, her people would find a way to take back what was theirs.

"I have kept in touch with her over the years. After her husband died, she took up his practice and she began teaching all of the traditional ways. She insisted that her children learn to read and write in their traditional language first, then in English. She met great resistance from the settlers, who were trying to change the Sioux.

"Her children are grown, and she now lives on the Rosebud Indian Reservation, or I thought she did. I heard recently that she was sick and had decided to go and find her original people—the people who had left her in the forest where she was found and adopted by the Sioux."

"She was adopted?" I said

"Oh, yes," said Grandma. "She was found by a Sioux warrior returning from battle. He saw no one around and did not know what group she belonged to. He brought her back to be raised by his family. Her Sioux sister was just a year old at the time."

"So we are trying to find her now because she may be sick, Grandma?" I asked.

"Yes, Rufus," said Grandma. "We are going to Rosebud Indian Reservation. My friend, George Pote, thinks there is a man there who knows where she was heading."

As we had been talking, the snow had been falling faster and thicker. It was piling up on the roadside. In the distance the land was no longer flat.

"Are those mountains?" I asked Grandma.

"They are hills, Rufus," Grandma said. "As we get farther into South Dakota, thee will begin to see the Rocky Mountains."

A NEW FRIEND

As we drove along, the snow was blowing lightly across the road. There was a kind of whistling sound; it made me feel cold inside. After a while, it started to get dark, and Grandma said, "I'm getting kind of tired. I think we will stop in Sioux Falls for the night."

Sioux Falls did not look much like Ames. There seemed to be a lot of tall buildings, maybe five or six stories high, kind of crowded together. On some of the streets, the sidewalks were still wooden. There weren't as many trees as in Ames, and the streets were not as wide.

Grandma drove up and down, looking for a hotel. Finally, she said, "That looks okay," and we pulled in front of a big door. "Come with me, Rufus."

We got out of the car and went through the double doors into a big room with a counter. Through an archway there was a huge living room where a cowboy in a big hat was smoking a cigar and reading a newspaper.

I walked with Grandma up to the counter. She told a man behind the counter we needed a room for tonight.

"Do you want a room or suite?" he asked.

Grandma looked around as if she was sizing the place up. It looked kind of old-fashioned even to me.

"We will need our own bathroom."

"You'll be needing a suite, then," said the man behind the counter. "Is it just for one night?"

"Yes," said Grandma. "We also need laundry service, and we need our clothing by midmorning."

"Hmm," said the man. "That may cost a bit. I'll have to send it out. Can you have it ready in, say, half an hour?"

"I think so," said Grandma. "My car's out front." She started to hand the man the keys to the car. Then she remembered: "Barclay!" she said.

"Who's Barclay?" said the man.

"He's our dog," said Grandma. "We'll have to get him out of the car first. And could we have our bags brought up?"

"Sure," said the man. "But there'll be an extra charge for the dog, a deposit."

Grandma looked surprised. "Well, how much will that be?" she asked.

"Ten dollars," said the man.

"That's more than the room costs!" said Grandma. "But we'll pay it; we don't leave Barclay in the car. Come on, Rufus; let's get Barclay."

When we got to the car and I opened the door, I suddenly remembered that we'd been playing in the snow and the mud with Barclay the day before. Now he wasn't as grubby as Grandma and I were, but he was covered with mud.

"Oh, boy," I said. "Grandma, you and I have to do something about Barclay; he's a mess." Grandma came around the car and took a good look at Barclay, and then she headed back into the hotel, telling me to wait right there.

Barclay and I stood there for what seemed like forever. Finally, Grandma came out with two towels and a broom. She said, "Rufus and Barclay, follow me." We went down the street a little way between the door and where a man was shining shoes for people. And Grandma said, "Now, hold Barclay still." And she started to sweep him.

I don't think Barclay liked being swept with the broom, because he kept shaking all over every few minutes and the dust would fly every which way.

The cowboy with the big hat was having his boots shined, and I heard him say, "You got any waterproof stuff, boy?" The guy shining shoes didn't look like a boy. He was a grown-up, like my dad.

As soon as the cowboy left, the man who'd been shining the shoes came over and said, "Let me help you." He had an old brush with him. "We can use this and maybe brush some of that mud out." He bent down and gave Barclay a friendly pat on the head. He started to brush Barclay from his head down to his tail. Now Barclay was wagging his tail and not shaking so much. Then the man took one of the towels, rubbed Barclay all over, and wiped his nose and ears.

"Now," he said, "young fellow, don't you look so handsome!"

Barclay gave him a lick on the chin and sat down and held up a paw. Grandma was delighted and offered the man a dollar, but he said, "No, thank you. It was a pleasure."

Grandma argued with him a little bit, but he refused her money. They talked and joked for a while. Then we took Barclay and went into the hotel. He walked with his head held high, like he didn't feel like apologizing to anyone.

By this time, Grandma said, almost half an hour had passed. Grandma went to the desk and asked for the room key and a laundry bag. We walked up two flights of stairs and found our room. When we opened the door there was a sitting room, a bedroom with two big beds and a big bathroom with a claw-foot tub. Grandma told me to go into the bathroom, get out of my dirty clothes, and put my bathrobe on right away so she could send our dirty clothes to the laundry. When I came out of the bathroom, the clothes she had been wearing were already in the bag, and she had her bathrobe on. She placed the bag with all our clothes outside the door and called on the telephone to someone to come and get the bag.

"Okay, Rufus," she said. "Thee go and take a bath and get all clean. I'll get some clothes ready for thee. We're going to go out for dinner."

When I came out of the bathroom, Grandma had my good clothes laid out on one of the beds.

"Look what I found in thy suitcase," she said. There on the bed was Raggedy Andy. "I guess Emily wanted thee to have him for the trip," she said. "We will send him back when we get to Bellingham.

"Now get into thy clothes while I get cleaned up, and wait for me in the sitting room," said Grandma.

I sat in the sitting room, where I found some little magazines with lots of pictures of cowboys and buildings and things that looked like they were part of the town we were in. When Grandma came out, she was wearing her old gray dress and her bonnet. I was a little disappointed after seeing her in Grandpa's overalls. I thought maybe she should wear some more of Grandpa's clothes. That would've been a lot more interesting.

"Well, let's go find someplace to eat," said Grandma. So we went back down onto the sidewalk. The man who had been shining shoes was already gone. We just walked down the street, looking for someplace to eat. Finally, Grandma saw a place with a sign that read, "Diner."

"Well, this will have to do," she said.

We went inside and sat down. Pretty soon, a lady in an apron came and brought us some pieces of paper that had writing on them. Grandma asked me what I would like to eat.

"Dinner," I said. I wasn't being a smart aleck; I had never been in a restaurant before. I had never eaten anywhere except home or at a Friend's house.

"Okay," said Grandma, "but what food would thee like for dinner?"

"What are they having?" I asked.

"Oh," she said, "thee can ask them for anything thee wants, and they fix it for thee."

"Really?" I said. "I can have anything I want?"

"No," she said, "thee has to have something that's good for thee."

"Okay," I said, "how about turkey with dressing and cranberry sauce?"

"Well, I'll have to see if it's on the menu," said Grandma.

"I thought you said I could have anything I wanted."

Grandma sighed.

"Why don't I just give thee a couple of choices? Would thee like chicken or meatballs?"

I had to think about it for a few minutes. "Okay," I said, "meatballs with spaghetti and maybe some salad and a glass of milk."

Grandma said, "I think I'll have the same thing and maybe a cup of tea." When the lady with the apron came back, that's what Grandma told her. She went away, and not very long after that she came back with our dinner.

It wasn't as good as Cora's cooking; it was okay because we were really hungry. After that, I started to clean up my place at the table. Grandma said I didn't need to do that this time, that the lady in the apron got paid to do that. Besides, Grandma left some extra money on the table for her.

We got up and paid some more money to a man at the counter, and then we went back to the hotel. We got to sleep in the two big beds, and the next morning we got to have breakfast at the hotel. The man with the cowboy hat was there too. He was talking with some of his friends in a loud voice—something about cows and corn.

As we were paying for our breakfast, Grandma asked for a doughnut and large cup of coffee to go.

"We don't have to-go cups," said the woman who was taking her money. "I can sell you a melamine cup with a lid for twenty-five cents."

"All right." Grandma sighed. She turned to me. "Now, Rufus, I want thee to take this to the kind man who helped Barclay last night. I will make some calls and meet thee by the front door."

I found the front door, and when I got outside, it was cold and a wind was blowing. The shoeshine man was sitting on his stool kind of hunched over, trying to keep warm, I think.

"Hi," I said. "Grandma and I thought you might like some coffee and a doughnut. We have to leave today and go look for Grandma's friend in South Dakota."

"Why, thank you, young man," he said. "How old are you?"

"Oh, sorry," I said, thinking I had forgotten my manners. I put out my hand. "I'm Rufus Thomas, and I am almost six years old. How old are you?"

He laughed, shook my hand, and said, "Well, I'm Miles Washington, and I am thirty-eight years old. You certainly are smart for your age!"

I didn't know what to say. I thought it was right to say something nice about him. "You are nice for your age, Miles Washington," I said. That didn't seem quite right. But he did laugh, so I guess he wasn't mad.

He said, "You and your grandma have a wonderful trip, and I sure hope she finds her friend."

"Take care of thyself, Friend Miles Washington," I said, not realizing at the time I was talking just like Grandma. For some reason, this conversation made me feel important and like I had made a new friend.

Grandma went to a pay phone and called the moving company again, and then she called a friend of hers in South Dakota. She told me her friend George Pote, who she wanted to visit on the way to the reservation, was an animal doctor, and lived in Pierre.

When we got back to our room, our clothes were hanging on the door on hangers. It looked like they had pressed our overalls and even our long underwear. Grandma put them neatly in our suitcases. Barclay was eager to see us and seemed really like he wanted to get on the road.

Grandma said, "I think Barclay needs to use the bathroom."

I looked around. I didn't think Barclay could use the bathroom, and I hadn't seen any grass outside.

"I think we need to take Barclay to the country somewhere," I told Grandma.

"Or at least the park," said Grandma. "Look around the room and make sure thee hasn't forgotten anything, especially Raggedy Andy, and then I think we should get going."

Grandma called somebody on the phone and said that we needed our car brought up. We went downstairs and paid the bill, and our car was right there at the door. Somebody got our bags. This was all new to me: not having to do things for ourselves.

As we were driving out of town, we went by a garage—the kind of place where they fix cars.

"Some people at the Nelsons' said we should get cables or something to wrap around the tires," said Grandma, "but I don't know what they mean. I've never driven through this part of the country in the wintertime." She stopped at the garage and asked somebody about the cables. They said they were all out of chains.

"Oh, well," said Grandma, "we'll just have to do without."

When we got out into the country a way, we stopped, tied the rope around Barclay's collar, and let him out of the car so he could go to the bathroom. Barclay, of course, wanted to smell everything. It was starting to snow harder by then, so Grandma insisted that he get back in the car and we started out again.

AN EMERGENCY

*I*know that I was thinking things over, because after a while I asked, "Do you think Miles Washington likes shining shoes, Grandma?"

"What does thee think, Rufus?" Grandma replied.

I had been thinking a lot about Miles Washington. When he was helping Barclay, he seemed really happy. It made me feel happy too.

"I think he liked brushing Barclay better. Sometimes he looks really sad when he is shining shoes. Sometimes he sings, like he is trying to cheer up. This morning it was really cold, but he was still there," I said.

"I think it's the only job he can get," she said, and she sounded sad.

"Why?" I asked. "He is smart, and I think he would rather work with animals."

"Because he's colored," Grandma replied.

"What did he color?" I asked, thinking of the time I had to sit in the corner, when I wrote on the wall.

"No, I mean it is hard right now to get a job if you are not a white person," she said.

I had to think about that, I had no idea who these "white" people were. Maybe she meant people with white hair. "You mean like Grandpa?" I said.

"Rufus. Don't be silly!" She was getting frustrated.

"Silly?" I said.

We were both quiet for a few minutes; then Grandma started laughing. I started giggling, too, although I wasn't sure why.

"Grandma," I said, "I've never seen a white person."

"I know," she said. "When I figure it out, I will explain it to thee."

We both giggled about that for a while, off and on. And I also kept thinking of ways that I could help Miles Washington to do what would make him happy.

It seemed to be snowing harder, and the road was getting a little hillier. We came to a place where our road ended, and we had to turn one way or the other. There were no signs to tell us which road we were on, or even where they were going.

"Where are we, Grandma?" I asked.

"Lost," she said, "but we have to pick a road, and hopefully we will find out where we are when we get there."

"Okay," I said. So we turned one way. It looked like a wider road. Pretty soon the snow was coming down so thick and fast that we could barely see beyond the front of the car. We drove on like this, carefully, for quite a while. Grandma would roll down the window and check for a mailboxes and poles at the side of the road, to let her know that she was still on the road.

After a long time, I said. "Is this Fifth Day or Sixth Day?"

"It's only Fourth Day, Rufus," said Grandma. "You know, I think it is time for thee to learn the names for the days of the week, because hardly anyone uses the Quaker names in the real world these days."

"The Real World," I said with a laugh. "Okay."

"So, starting with First Day; it's Sunday, Monday, and Tuesday . . ."

"Sunday, Mon—," I started to repeat.

Just then, the car started spinning in circles. I slid across the seat and almost into Grandma's lap. Barclay fell off the back seat and landed on the floor with a yelp and a thud. (Cars didn't have seat belts then).

"Mother of God!" Grandma whispered, loudly.

And the windshield in front of us went all white. The car stopped.

"Is thee all right, Rufus?" she asked, reaching out to me.

"Yes," I said. "But does God have a mother?"

Grandma looked a little confused. She rubbed her forehead. She looked over at me and said, "Is thee ever afraid, Rufus?"

"Oh, yes," I replied. "What happened?"

"We crashed into a snowbank, I think," said Grandma.

I pulled up on the handle and pushed on my door. It wouldn't budge. Now, I was feeling really scared. We could hear Barclay crying from the floor in back.

"Climb in back and try the back doors," said Grandma. "Be careful not to step on Barclay. I think he's hurt."

I crawled over the front seat in the middle and jumped onto the back seat. The door on Grandma's side, where Barclay was lying, wouldn't budge, but the one on my side opened easily.

"It opens, Grandma," I said.

"Now go out and look around, and see if thee can see anyone," said Grandma.

I walked out, through the deep snow, to the edge of the road and looked up and down. The road stretched out straight for a long way. There were high snowbanks on either side, but no cars and no people. I listened and I could hear no one. It was very quiet.

Then I remembered something that Grandpa showed me, when we got the car, the summer before. I hurried back and opened the car door.

"Grandma," I said, "is this a 'mergency?"

"Yes, Rufus. It certainly is," said Grandma.

"Look under my seat," I said with a smile. "There's a box there that Grandpa said was for 'mergencies."

Grandma leaned over and pulled what looked like a small suitcase from under the seat. She placed it on my seat and opened it. She pulled out a flashlight and turned it on. Then she pulled out a couple more things.

"Rufus," she said, "does thee know how to light matches?"

"Well, I never did it," I lied, "but I've seen you do it lots of times."

She handed me a small tin and a large cylinder. "I'm so glad thee remembered this box, Rufus," she said. "Now listen carefully: I want thee to light a match and then light the flag on the top of this rocket. First put the rocket in the middle of the road, right in back of the car. Is the car off the road?"

"Yes, it's way off the road," I said.

"Good." she said. "After thee lights the little flag, stand back. It's going to make a big light and fire that people can see for quite a ways. That way, maybe someone will come and help us."

I didn't tell Grandma I knew how to light matches because I wasn't supposed to play with them. She was right, though, the flare did make a pretty big light up in the air. I came back to the car, and we shined the flashlight on Barclay to see what was wrong. He looked up at us but didn't move much. He whimpered.

"He might've broken something," said Grandma. "Let's find a blanket to put over him. I don't think we should move him. I wish I knew where we were. If we're close to Pierre, maybe my friend George Pote could take a look at him."

Just then, there was a tap on the window. It scared me a little. Grandma said, "Open the door; someone's here."

The light we put out must've helped someone find us! I opened the door. A man in a big yellow jacket was standing there.

"Hi! I work for the county," he said. "Looks like you're having some trouble here."

"Well," Grandma said. "I think maybe we ran off the road into a snowbank, and our dog is hurt. Can thee pull us out of here? Where are we, anyway?"

"I'm the snowplow driver," said the man in the yellow jacket. "I can't pull you out, but I can radio the garage down the road about a mile. And George Pote is about the best animal doc in the Dakotas. He is only about ten miles from here. Where you are is almost in the Missouri River. Good thing there's a snowbank here."

"George Pote!" exclaimed Grandma. "He's the friend we are going to visit."

"Well, that's good," said the county man. "I'll just have Mike at the garage give him a call and let him know you're here. Lucky for you that snowbank was here, or you'd both be swimming," he added with a laugh. "You might as well stay right here in the car where it's nice and warm." And he walked off toward the road.

It didn't seem very long until the tow truck arrived, and also the man named Mike with a shovel. He started digging around the front by Grandma's door and under the car. Pretty soon they had a chain around the back axle, and Mike said they were going to try to pull the car out a little way.

"We need to see what kind of damage there might be," he said, "before we put it on the road."

The car moved and snow fell from the top. It slid out far enough so that daylight came in our windows. Mike came to Grandma's door and brushed the snow off. Then he slowly opened her door.

"Let's have you and the boy get out, and we'll pull it out onto the road. Then we can get a good look underneath and see if anything's broken before we tow it," Mike told Grandma.

"Our dog is lying on the back floor," said Grandma. "I don't know if we should take him out. Something might be broken. I don't know whether to move him."

Just then a panel truck with a picture of a horse and a dog pulled up.

"Well, that's George now," said Mike. "I think he can help us with that problem."

George Pote got out of his truck, rushed over to Grandma, and gave her a big hug.

"Now where's that dog of yours?" he said.

Grandma opened the back door of the car, and Barclay tried to get up and let out a loud yelp.

"Don't move, boy," said George Pote. "We're going to help you out. Stay." Barclay gave a sigh and lay back down.

George went back to his truck and got out a small board that was padded with something. He climbed into the back seat and told me to stand in the door and hold the board for him. Then he took one end of the board and slid it under Barclay from the front and said, "Hold it underneath him."

Barclay whimpered.

When George Pote got it all the way under the dog, he said, "Now hold that end real steady and pull it out, while I push."

When he got out of the car, he was carrying Barclay. He took him, on the board, to his truck. By the time he got there, they had our car out in the road.

Mike said, "I don't see anything important broken under there, but I can't seem to get it started. So I think we need to tow it back to the shop. It might just be frozen up. At any rate, you need some chains on those tires."

"I tried to get some in Sioux Falls, but they were all out," Grandma said. "I'm glad you have some."

George Pote walked over from his truck to where we were standing. "Liz, you and Rufus should come with me; we can pick your car up in the morning."

"Do you have room for us in that thing?" asked Grandma. She got our suitcases out of the car, and we got into the front seat of George's truck. I could hear Barclay snoring in the back. I looked at George Pote. I was surprised.

"Oh, I gave him some medicine for his pain; he is quite comfortable right now," said George. "When we get him back to the clinic, I'll set that leg of his. It seems to be broken. And I'll give him a good checkup. I bet you are hungry. I have a good dinner in the oven."

We followed the tow truck for a little while, until they pulled into the garage. George Pote honked his horn as we went by.

"Don't worry about your car; they will take good care of it," he said to Grandma.

For the rest of the way to the animal clinic, he and Grandma talked about all kinds of things from the old days, and I almost fell asleep.

BARCLAY'S RECOVERY

George Pote's clinic was hooked right onto his house. He carried Barclay on the board into his office. He had an assistant who helped him fix Barclay's leg, and they gave Barclay some more medicine to help him sleep. They put a cast on Barclay's front leg and put him in a kind of cage, with some soft blankets and things, so he wouldn't try to walk if he woke up.

"He's going to sleep for a while," said George Pote. "Why don't we go and get some dinner?"

Dinner was some really good beans and cornbread that had been cooking in the oven most of the day. After dinner, Grandma and George Pote talked about how Grandma was going to find her friend, and how to get to Rosebud Reservation. George said there was a fellow in Rosebud who might know where Grandma's friend had gone. But he also said it wasn't the best weather to try to go down there; the roads weren't very good this time of year, and the snow was drifting.

Grandma seemed very determined to find her friend and didn't seem to care about the weather. George Pote had a couple of maps, and they started drawing lines on them and looking at them carefully. He made some phone calls and was asking people about the roads. George Pote seemed to know everybody in the whole state of South Dakota.

Finally, he said, "Okay, Liz, if you're going to go, this is the way you need to do it." And they talked about the roads and drew on his map.

Grandma also told George and me another thing about her friend Sunshine, something that she hadn't told me before. Sunshine had been adopted by a Sioux family after she was found alone in the forest on her cradleboard hanging in a tree. Everyone thought that something terrible had happened to her mother and that she left Sunshine, hoping that someone would find her. Now Sunshine had left her home to try to find out who her mother's people had been.

When it was time to go to bed, I said I wanted to sleep with Barclay.

George said, "It's pretty cold out there in the kennel. And I really don't want to move Barclay. How about you sleep here in the living room, and we'll leave the door to the clinic open so you can hear Barclay if he wakes up."

Well, I thought that was okay, because I could sneak out and look at Barclay once in a while. George got me a blanket and some pillows, and I lay down on the couch. The adults were still talking when I fell asleep.

I guess Barclay didn't wake up that night, because it was daylight when I woke up and the house was quiet. I got up and quietly went into the clinic and into the back area, and there was Barclay, snoring away on his soft blankets in his kennel. He looked funny with that big white cast on his leg. I called his name and he made a little noise in his sleep, but he didn't open his eyes.

When I got back into the house, George Pote was making coffee. Grandma must've still been asleep.

"Want some pancakes?" George asked. "And maybe a glass of orange juice?"

"Okay," I said. "Barclay's still asleep—he doesn't seem to be in pain. Will he be able to walk?"

"Yes, but I don't want him walking on that leg very much for a few days," said George. "We want the bone to start mending before he puts any weight on it."

"Boy," I said. "I think Grandma wants to get going pretty soon. She really wants to find that friend of hers."

"I know; your grandma is pretty stubborn," said George. "Maybe Barclay can stay here with me for a few days. You'll have to come back this way anyway. I think your grandma is pretty tired. She's snoring away just like Barclay."

I laughed at that. "Grandma can sure snore," I said. "She must be tired, though; she's done a lot lately."

I ate my pancakes, drank my juice, and then put my dishes in the sink.

George Pote asked me if I knew how to play checkers. I said I didn't, and he said, "Well, then, I'll teach you."

So we sat down and I learned how to play checkers, and we played checkers for what seemed like a very long time. After a while, I think I won one.

"Good morning," said Grandma. "How long did I sleep? What time is it?"

I smiled up at her and said, "Dinnertime, of course. Barclay's sleeping just fine and he doesn't seem to be in any pain and I learned how to play checkers and George says he needs to stay here for a couple days because he can't walk on his leg, and I think we should stay a little while, too, because I think you need rest, and it's awfully snowy out there."

"Boy, thee sure has a lot of opinions," said Grandma. "Now what time is it really? For one thing I have to find out about the car, and then we have to find out how long it's going to take us to get to Rosebud and if we have enough time to go there today."

George turned around and looked at the clock. "It's 11:15," he said. "I will call Mike and find out about the car. Why don't you two go check on Barclay and then have some coffee?"

Barclay was stirring in his kennel and slowly trying to find his tail. He wasn't used to having that thing on his leg, and he looked kind of funny trying to turn a circle, although he wasn't standing.

The assistant was there by then, and she thought maybe he needed some water so she gave me a bowl. I took him the water and I sat down on the blanket next to him and patted him on the head. He looked at me, giving me kind of a silly look, and then he licked my hand.

"He is going to be just fine," the assistant said." We may keep him kind of drowsy for a few days so he doesn't walk around very much."

George Pote came in and told Grandma, "Mike's going to bring your car by in a few minutes. He said the battery died and he needed to give it a jumpstart. He wants to know: do you want a new battery? He says the one you've got will probably last you until you get to Seattle at least, but he'll put a new one in if you want."

Grandma said, "Let's be safe and put a new one in. I don't want to have any trouble on the top of some mountain or something."

"Okay," George said. "I'll call him back. We also need to figure out how long it will take you to get to Rosebud and whether there's any place for you to stay down there, or if you need to make the trip in one day."

"Grandma," I said, "maybe we should just go tomorrow."

"Rufus," said Grandma, kind of sternly, "thee is getting just a little bit too grown-up. And I think thee worries too much. Will thee leave that up to me?" Then she gave me that familiar smile.

Grandma went outside for a while. When she came back, she said, "Well, Rufus, I think it *is* a better idea if we go tomorrow, if George doesn't mind keeping us for one more day." She turned to George, who smiled in response.

"I need to call the moving company," she said. "I am sure we won't be getting to Washington by the second. And I should go into town to the bank this afternoon. Is it okay if I leave Rufus here with thee for a bit?

"Oh, yes," said George Pote. "It'll give me a chance to beat him at checkers again."

Grandma came back and said, "The moving company says that someone has to be there to sign off for the furniture. So I'll have to see if I can get my brother to do it.

I'll have to send him the inventory. I hope it gets there in time.

"They won't forget Thomas B, will they?" I said.

"I will let thee talk to thy great-uncle and tell him to watch for Thomas B," Grandma assured me. I think she was beginning to understand how important it was to me.

❦

When George Pote got out the checkerboard and we started playing checkers, I thought maybe he would know how I could find out something. I had been wondering about it a lot since we left Sioux Falls.

"Do you know if they make brushes," I asked, "just for dogs?" I wondered because I wanted to get one for Miles Washington. I thought maybe if he could get a job brushing dogs, he would be happier.

"Well, I have a special steel comb," George said, "that I use to get burrs out when dogs get into something or get injured. Some people who show their dogs in dog shows have special brushes for their dogs. Are you thinking of getting a brush for Barclay?"

"No," I said, "I have a friend who likes to brush dogs."

"Oh," said George Pote.

I thought about how happy and proud Barclay seemed after he got brushed. He held his head up and walked so briskly into that hotel. It seemed to me that lots of people would want to have their dogs brushed. Whenever I thought about that, I wanted to smile.

I didn't win very many checker games because my mind was on other things. Before long, it was getting dark.

Grandma came back with some milk and cookies, and a feed sack stuffed with sawdust for Barclay's new bed in the car. "Now he will have something soft on the floor so he won't slide off the seat and fall again," she said.

She had some other groceries and told George Pote that she would make dinner, so he went to check on Barclay.

After a few minutes George came back carrying the dog, who was awake enough to be looking around. I put Barclay's new bed in front of the woodstove, and he tried to prop himself up on his front legs. The cast was a little awkward, so George got him a pillow. He lay there, wagging his tail. It was his way of smiling.

I asked George a lot of questions about the kinds of things he did in his clinic. I learned that he took care of a lot of farm animals.

After a while, Grandma said, "Thee might have noticed that this boy likes to ask questions."

That reminded me that we still hadn't finished our conversation about Miles Washington and she hadn't answered my question about God's mother.

"Grandma," I said. "You never told me where these white people are. I've never seen one."

"What?!" said George Pote.

"Yeah," I said. "Grandma said it's real hard to get a job now unless you're a white person. That's why my friend Miles Washington shines shoes."

I looked at Grandma to see if she would explain, but she didn't say anything, so I went on.

"She says Miles Washington is 'colored.' But we're *all* colored. I'm kinda light tan and Grandpa is kinda dark tan and Bill

Scott is kinda reddish-pinkish tan and Miles Washington is dark brown, and we're all some kinda colored. None of us seem to be quite the same. But I have never seen a white person. In the summer, I get brown spots on my face and arms. So does Bill."

Grandma looked at George Pote and said, "Well, he is right of course, but how do I explain all this?"

"You' re right, Rufus," said George Pote. "No one is actually white. All people have different colors of skin. As a matter of fact, everyone is different from everyone else. It's not just the color of our skin, but the color of our eyes and the size of our teeth, even how big our little toes are. All of these things are different in each person; we get a little bit of everything from our parents. They got a little bit of everything from *their* parents. And it goes back through parents for a long time. So probably you had parents and grandparents and great-grandparents with lighter-colored skin. Miles Washington probably had parents and grandparents and great-grandparents with darker-colored skin.

"Even though we are all different from one another, we have many things in common—very many things that we all share. In nature, it is not important what the color of your skin is or the color of your eyes. It might be more important how fast you can run, or how strong you are.

"The problem for some people is that they have prejudice. That means that some people don't like people who are different. Sometimes people make it hard for people who look different or sound different or have different beliefs from them.

"It's more complicated than that, but maybe it's not in some ways. Miles Washington has trouble getting a job because of prejudice. Not because he isn't smart or because he wants to shine shoes. Maybe he would like to work with animals, and maybe no one wants to hire him to do that. I don't know Miles Washington, so I don't know exactly why he hasn't found a different job. But I think it's probably because of prejudice."

I sighed.

"Okay, then, who are these white people who are getting jobs?" I had a feeling this was one of those things that grown-ups do that makes no sense.

"Oh, dear," said Grandma. "I'm thinking that this is one of those things that children are smarter about."

"What do you mean?" I asked.

Grandma and George Pote looked at each other.

"Well, to be honest," Grandma said, "people who have ancestors who came from Europe, like we do, have gotten in the habit of calling ourselves 'white people' and everyone else something else. Probably because some people with ancestors from Europe think white is a better color. We aren't really white, just a lighter skin color."

I laughed, but Grandma and George Pote didn't think it was funny. So I asked, "Why?"

"Hmm," said Grandma. "Maybe some people think we are better than everyone else? Or maybe we want to make sure we know we are different than people from some other place?"

"So we are not from America?" I said. "Mum's not from America, and I guess I'm not, really. But I feel like I am. Is anyone from America?"

"Well, yes, some people's ancestors were here when the very first Europeans came, a long time ago. My friend, who I am looking for, is Sioux. Her people are from America," Grandma said.

"Is she white?" I asked.

"No," Grandma said. "We call her 'Indian,' although she was raised in the Sioux Nation."

"Okay," I said. "So why does all this make it hard to get a job, if you're not white?"

"Discrimination," said George Pote. "That means that some people don't like other people just because of the color of their skin, so they won't give them a job."

I was beginning to feel really strange. I wondered if this was some kind of strange story. It made no sense, but I had a sick feeling that it might be true.

"That's stupid!" I yelled. And then I realized that I had yelled at an adult.

"I'm sorry, George Pote," I said. "I didn't mean to be rude; I was just . . . um . . . I just didn't believe it . . . I mean . . ." And then I started crying because I thought I was in trouble.

Both George and Grandma each put an arm around me. "That's okay, Rufus," Grandma said. "Thee is right to feel upset about that! It is wrong that people treat other people that way in this country."

"What can we do, Grandma?" I asked. Then I had a really good idea. "Maybe George Pote could hire Miles Washington, and then he could work with animals."

So Grandma and I told George all about Miles and how he helped with Barclay and how I thought he would love to work with animals.

"And he's really good with them," I said.

"You know, that is a fine idea, Rufus," said George, "and I sure would hire him. The thing is, I only hired Alice for a few hours after school, and I don't pay her much. The truth is, I don't really have a big enough practice. You know there are a lot of fellows just like Miles Washington. We have to do more to make things fair for Miles and to have more jobs for people like Miles, who have such good skills that aren't getting used. He might even be a good vet, but he probably doesn't have a chance to go to school. And I bet he has a family to support."

"What can we do, Grandma?" I pleaded.

"Let's find out what more we can do. Let's talk to Grandpa about this," Grandma tried to reassure me. "I think he may know some ways that we can help to make things fairer for people."

That sounded nice, but I was still thinking that there were a lot of things that I didn't understand. "I'm pretty tired," I said. "Can we save my question about God's mother until later?"

"Oh, yes. Please," said Grandma.

⚜

I lay down with my pillow and blanket and turned to face the back of the couch. I tried to fall asleep. I was very tired. Grandma and George Pote were still at the table, talking.

I heard a little bit of what they were saying. Grandma thought maybe I was taking on too much for such a little boy. George said perhaps I just wanted to learn things. Then they started to talk about people—not certain people, but all people—and how things weren't fair. They were using a lot of words that I didn't understand.

At one point, Grandma said, "Rufus wants to save the world." But I think she had it wrong. I wanted to help Miles Washington. *She* wanted to save the world. Maybe I didn't even so much want to help Miles Washington as I just wanted him to be happy.

After a while the murmur of their voices put me to sleep.

⚜

The sun coming in the kitchen window and the sound of a cat meowing woke me early the next morning. When I looked out the window, it was mostly covered with ice.

George Pote must have heard me get up, because he was standing behind me in his robe.

"Let's have some breakfast," he said. "You and your grand-mother should be on the road soon if you mean to get to Rosebud in good time today."

"Okay," I said. "How is Barclay?"

On hearing his name Barclay rolled over in his bed by the fire and looked at me. I got him a little water and brought the bowl over to him. He managed to get up on three legs and drink.

"Good boy!" said George, and he gave Barclay a treat. Barclay wagged his tail. He thumped the cast down on the floor and then looked at it, startled. We both laughed.

Barclay held up his injured front leg and looked at me as if to say, *What's all this?*

Barclay finally managed to get turned around and fell back onto his bed with a heavy sigh.

Grandma came into the kitchen and poured herself some coffee. She sat at the table, smiling at Barclay.

George Pote put some canned food in a bowl and placed it a short distance from where the dog lay. Barclay looked up at him with the saddest eyes but didn't move.

"Okay," said George, "let's have some eggs and toast."

We sat at the table to eat, and I kept one eye on Barclay. He tried to get up, whined, and looked over at us. George touched my hand and shook his head. He wanted me to ignore the dog's pleading.

Pretty soon, Barclay managed to pull himself up on his three good legs. He hobbled to the food bowl, looking over at us and making quite a show of it. When he finished eating, he looked back at his bed, over at the table, and then back at his bed. Then he walked on all three legs and the cast, toward us. It was pretty noisy on the tile floor, but he made it, his tail wagging all the way. He licked Grandma's hand and looked up at her pleadingly.

"What a good boy," said Grandma. "Thee is going to be just fine."

We looked at him and praised him. I think he was proud and happy.

I explained to Barclay that we were going for a drive and would see him later. He didn't seem at all concerned. He curled up in his bed by the fire while Grandma and George Pote looked at the map that George had on the table.

They talked about which roads we should take and which detours to take, if they were closed. George told her where to stay if she couldn't get back to Pierre by nightfall.

ROSEBUD

George helped us out with our blankets and some extra food he had packed for us.

Grandma pulled out onto the road and looked at the directions that George Pote had carefully written out for her. She seemed more relaxed and like she knew where she was going.

"Is the place we are going an Indian village?" I asked, excited.

"A small village and an agency headquarters for the reservation," Grandma answered.

"Will there be teepees, and chiefs with feather headdresses and bows and arrows?" I asked. I had seen a movie about Indians once.

"No, Rufus," said Grandma. "It is nothing like the movies. There will probably be a few small buildings, maybe a school or a church."

"Oh," I said. "I thought Indians lived in teepees."

"Not anymore," she said.

We were both quiet for a long time after that. I was quiet at first because I was disappointed, and then I was thinking about what Indians might be like if they didn't live in teepees.

I think Grandma was thinking about her friend.

We traveled along for another hour or so. It was flat and the snow was blowing around on the highway. The sun was still kind of low and not real bright. I didn't see much of anything along the road. We saw a sign that Grandma read aloud: MURDO—2 MILES. We went through Murdo. It was small: some stores and houses, a gas station, and a motel. Then a sign said ROSEBUD, with an arrow showing which way to go. Another sign said BIA.

"What does that mean, Grandma?" I asked.

"Bureau of Indian Affairs. Well, it's sup-posed to mean the government helps the Indians. But they don't do a very good job of it."

"Oh," I said. I wasn't sure it was an answer, but like so many other things, it would have to do.

Soon we came to what looked like the end of the road. There was a row of small unpainted houses, one with a flag flying in front. A few of the houses had smoke coming from the chimneys.

Grandma had been wrong, however; at the end of the row and off a short distance were four teepees, grouped together, with light smoke coming from between the poles.

I looked at Grandma and nodded toward them and smiled. She smiled back, as if she was glad she'd been wrong.

We got out of the car. Standing right in front of the door of the building with the flag was an old woman. She was standing on one foot and then the other. She rubbed her hands together to keep them warm.

Grandmother came up beside her and said gently, "Thee should go inside; it is very cold out here."

"Can't you see I'm waiting in line for my rations?" the old woman shouted at her.

When I looked down, I noticed that the woman had a shoe that had no bottom on it. She was standing in the snow with her bare foot.

My grandmother put her arm around her shoulder and said to the people that neither of us could see, "Please let this grand-mother go first; she is cold and tired." And then she helped the woman into the building.

There was a long-haired man sitting behind the counter. I think he was asleep. He started when we walked in.

"Oh, Dora. We aren't doing rations anymore. The war is over," he said.

"I need lard and flour," said Dora. "I got no coal. No fire. Damn near froze las' night!"

"Everyone the same here, now," said the man. "First of the year we'll have more." The man sighed and turned his back.

"What about shoes?" Grandma said, nearly shouting at him.

I was surprised. She hardly ever raised her voice in anger at anyone.

"Sister," the man replied, "I am just a poor Indian. Agency people only come around when there's trouble to make. Just yesterday, I tied some sacks around that foot. She keeps pulling them off. She used to be one of our wisest elders. Her mind is gone. We love her. We try to help. We don't know what to do.

"Who is this boy?" He looked at me.

"I am a Quaker, not a nun," said Grandma. "He is my grand-son. Does Dora live alone?"

"Yes, her husband died last winter," said the man. "After that she went off. We need to find someone who she thinks needs her. But everyone here is families and already very crowded.

"Are you lost?" he asked.

"No, we are looking for a man that my friend calls 'The Blind Seer,'" said Grandma.

"Oh, yes!" said the man. "Agents call him Dark Dreamer, but that is an insult. His dreams are anything but dark. He helps people find their way. He is in one of the teepees. The agents do not like the teepees, so kindly do not mention them. They have a good purpose, as you will see. We call him 'Joe' now. That is the name they gave him at school."

As we were leaving, the man added, "I can give Dora some beans. That will help for a while. We will have more supplies after the first of the year. I will walk her home and then take you to meet Joe."

"Thank thee," said Grandma. "Is there any way we can help?"

"I'm sorry you're not a nun," he said. "Sometimes the Church sends food and used clothes. But then they try to make us do things like live in the cold houses."

We went out the front door and stopped at Dora's house, which was two doors away. The man helped her in the door, and she slammed it behind her.

Then he showed us to the teepee and held the flap open. He said something in Sioux and left us.

I was kind of amazed. I guess I thought it would be like a little camping tent. It was really big inside. A group of men and women sat around a fire in the very center of the teepee. Even at the edge it wasn't cold like outside. Grandma took my hand and said, "Just stand here until we are invited. Oh, and it is impolite for children to look directly at adults."

I thought that was really strange, as grown-ups were always saying, "Look at me when I talk to you," but I guessed this was some special rule.

After a very short time a woman said, "Come. Sit," and motioned to us.

So we went and sat down beside her with our legs crossed. People continued to talk a bit, mostly in English, and then everyone stopped and just looked at my grandmother. I remembered to look down.

Grandma said, "My friend George Pote sent me to find the answer to a question. The question is mine. I am searching for a friend."

"We know George; he understands animals and is our friend. This is your grandson? Would you like fry bread?" asked a man across the fire.

"Yes, yes," said Grandma quietly. "My friend said I should talk with a blind man who sees many things; he knows where my friend, whom I call Sunshine, has gone."

It seemed like everyone relaxed and started talking at once. The woman next to us broke off something that looked like a piece of pancake and handed it to Grandma, who handed me a piece. It tasted pretty good.

"We've wondered when you would come," the woman said. "We know who you're looking for and where she is headed. We know who you are. You're old Paul's daughter. We will let Joe tell you."

It turned out Joe was sitting right next to me. He was looking ahead and rocking a little.

"She came to me," he said. "She was living up in Pine Ridge a ways. She said that before she died, she wanted to find her people. I knew what she meant. She meant the people of her birth. This was not an easy thing for me to find. Your 'Sunshine' has a lot of anger hiding her being. And her stories are many. We had to meet many times until she could quiet herself so that we could listen. She is a spirit-filled woman, but it is very deep and private.

"Then one day she brought with her a cradleboard. I don't know where she had kept it. I'm sure the elders knew of it, but we had never seen it. It was one of those very beautifully decorated ones with a hood on top. Of course, I only felt it; she described it to me.

"We knew some of the nations who used cradleboards; this only gave a few hints. The thing is that I just knew. An image came to me of a great speechmaker. I told her that day, 'Your people are Chief Joseph's people. They are on the Colville Reservation out in Washington.' She said now she knew too. She seemed as sure as I was. I had to tell her one more thing. I said, 'I have seen that you have a fire in your breast.'"

Grandma said, "Yes, she has always had a passion for greatness!"

"No!" Joe exclaimed. "Not like a white man's saying. A real fire, and a sickness. She will have to see doctors and have it cut out. Or see a healer."

"She said she would live for a few more years," said Joe, "and this would be enough to find her people. I got mad at her, because I know she has more than that in her."

My grandma said, "I'll find her and set her straight."

Everyone laughed and said, "Good luck with that."

When I laughed, I looked around and at the fire. I noticed there were other children, and some of them had crawled closer to me.

What was burning in the fire was not logs. It looked like flat discs of grass. I whispered to a little girl, "What's that you're burning?"

"Dung," she whispered back.

"What's dung?" I whispered.

"Buffalo poop," said an older man, and everyone laughed.

Then Joe said, "We have a lot of dung, but it won't burn in the coal or wood stoves in the houses. The smoke is terrible. We put up our teepee, which is warmer anyway, and we can burn it on our fires and keep warm."

Grandma asked about Dora, but they said she wouldn't come because sometimes she thinks her husband is still in her house and she doesn't want to leave him.

Then everyone fell silent for a while, which was nice. After a while Grandma said, "How will I find Sunshine?"

Several of the older people made sounds like *hmm?* and cleared their throats.

After a while Joe said, "She left with her son, her grandson, and her grandson's wife. They were going to cross Wyoming, where we think she was found, and then go on through Montana and into Washington. The weather has been bad, and they went with horses. They had some money, but not much. The men talked of finding work as they went. I will try to see if I can 'find' them or even think of how they might have stopped. When can you come back? I need some time alone. There may be others here who can help us."

Everyone was quiet some more, and then Grandma said, "I think we will go to Murdo tonight and come back tomorrow. There are some things I need to do there. I wish my father were here—he might know how to help Dora—or that one of your great healers were here."

The old woman close to us sighed.

Joe stood and held out a hand. Grandma rose to her feet and clasped Joe's hand. "I thank thee, Friend. Will we find thee here tomorrow?"

"Yes, I will be here," he replied. "Go in peace."

The woman beside Grandma rose and walked out of the teepee with us. She stopped Grandma a short way from the tent.

"Do you know how he lost his eyesight?" she asked.

"I don't," said Grandma.

"About ten years ago, before the war, a man sold or gave him some bad booze. It poisoned him, nearly killed him. I think it was over in Sioux City. It was a white man. We were all so angry. The only thing is, that man drank the same stuff, and it *did* kill him. We try to keep booze off the res now. Some still go to town to drink. It's a shame."

I didn't know what booze was. Grandma explained to me. She said that native people had no experience with alcohol before Europeans brought it to America, and it really made them sick and crazy. It was one of the terrible things that was done to the Indians.

For me the trip to Rosebud was just another example of the world of adults that just didn't make sense. Why did they have these wooden shacks to live in that couldn't be heated when the teepees were warmer and easier to heat?

When we drove away from Rosebud, I could tell that my grandmother was angry. Then she started talking.

"The government made treaties. They are supposed to take care of those people. They took everything away from them—and then to leave them like this! I'm sorry, Rufus. I don't mean to upset thee. I just think it is wrong."

"Grandma," I said, "I think you know a lot more about things than I do. I just think about people I meet, like Dora. I don't understand everything you say. I know it's important, but sometimes it makes my head hurt. Can we get Dora some shoes and something to eat? That would make me feel better. Does that make sense?"

My grandma reached across the seat and squeezed my hand. "That would make me feel better too," she said.

By the time we got back to Murdo and found the motel, it was dark. The motel was not like the hotel in Sioux Falls. Our room was opened with a key from outdoors, and there were two beds and a bathroom. It smelled smoky.

We found someplace to have dinner and then went back and got into bed. There was a telephone on the bedside table. Grandma went through an operator and called George Pote and told him a lot about what happened in Rosebud. They talked for a long time. She asked about Barclay and told me he was doing a little better. Finally, I fell asleep.

I woke up in the middle of the night because the electric heater on the wall came on and made a loud humming. I think it was the fan. The coils were glowing red, and I lay there for a while, thinking about the big fire and sitting in the circle listening to everyone talking the day before. And I wondered what Grandma's father would have done to help Dora.

Grandma had to wake me in the morning. The room was nice and warm, and it made me extra sleepy.

"Rufus," she called. "We have to get up and look for some warm socks and boots for Dora."

I smiled and rubbed the sleep out of my eyes.

"Okay," I said. "But we don't know her size."

"I looked carefully yesterday," said Grandma. "Her feet are a little smaller than mine. If we get extra-thick socks to keep out the cold, it should be just right.

"And George is coming with some friends. A trucker accidentally killed an elk on the highway yesterday. They have cleaned it and are bringing it for the people at Rosebud. They can cook the meat for food. George is also bringing some C-Rations that were left at the German POW camp."

"What?" I asked.

"Leftover food," she said.

"Hmm," I said, kind of unsure. I didn't know what "POW" was, or "German" either. I thought the explanation might take more time than I wanted just then.

(Later I learned it was leftover food that had been for prisoners from the war who were in this country. They were German soldiers who had been captured by Americans during the war. By the time Grandma and I were at Rosebud, they had been returned home. So the food was available for a good cause.)

We went to the general store, and Grandma bought some wool socks and a pair of work boots. Then we went to the grocery store where she bought three boxes of oranges. They only had three boxes. The man at the store said that was a lot and the price was high.

Grandma said, "Early Christmas present for fifty friends."

I asked Grandma if they had a dog brush, and she said she didn't think so, that it wasn't something people here would use. I really wanted to find one to send to Miles Washington.

We headed down the road; Grandma seemed in a hurry.

"Grandma, I'm hungry," I said.

"Oh, I forgot," she said. She turned around, went back to the diner, ran in, and came back with two rolls and two cups of coffee.

That was the first time I ever drank coffee. I don't think my Grandmother was really paying attention to much other than her concern about Rosebud that morning.

When we arrived, I was surprised to see that George was already there with his truck. People were gathered around his truck, and he was handing out boxes of supplies. Over by the teepees, some men were cutting up the elk meat.

Grandma took the oranges out of the car and placed the boxes in the snow next to George's truck. We took the package with the boots and socks into the office.

The same man was there as the day before. "We brought something for Dora's feet," Grandma told him.

"Good luck with that," he said. "She has been in her house, yelling all morning. She won't come out to get the food. She says it's all a lie."

"Why won't she go into the teepee, where it is warm?" asked Grandma.

"Because she won't leave her husband," he said. "And when she did go in there, no one else could see her husband, and she said they disrespected him."

We could hear her shouting from the office, although we couldn't hear what she was saying.

"Oh, my," said Grandma. "And starving can't be helping her mind much either."

She was quiet for a minute, then said, "I have an idea." She went to talk to George. She came back with two packets of food and a can opener.

"Now I want thee to play along with me, Rufus. Thee is a smart boy, so I know thee can do it," she said firmly, looking at me. "We do not know that her husband's spirit is not with her. She may not be wrong. So we are not really lying, we are respecting the spirit within her. Does thee understand this?"

I thought it was nice that Grandma trusted me, and I almost understood what she meant. I did know that it had something to do with respect. I did understand respect.

Grandma knocked on the door. Dora pulled the curtain aside and said, "What do you want, Sister?"

"I have food for you and your husband," my grandmother said in a rather official-sounding voice. I thought it was amazing that Grandma remembered to say "you" and not "thee." I think she was pretending to be a nun so Dora would accept the food and shoes.

"Well, it's about time," yelled the old woman. "Come in, then."

Grandma walked in and set the packages down on the table. "And also, the boots that you ordered last fall; we just got your size."

"Hmph," the old woman replied. Then she called something in Sioux toward a back room. "Well, they finally brought our food; come and sit and eat," she called out in English.

Grandma waited a minute or so and spoke in the direction of the back area: "Well, hello! Good to see you again." She made what I guess was a greeting in Sioux.

"And they finally got me shoes. You think they could get an old woman shoes before her feet freeze up," Dora said to her husband.

Turning toward Grandma, she shouted, "So when the hell are we going to get some wood or coal out here?"

"Dora, there are children present," said Grandma.

"Yeah, sorry," said Dora, glancing toward me.

"Maybe later this week," said Grandma. "They are burning dung in the teepee."

"I don't need that shi—sorry. And those Indians are disrespectful," said Dora. "Just because Lyle is dead is no reason to treat him with disrespect."

Grandma looked really surprised. She looked at me. I think she might have been confused.

"Maybe they can't see him?" I said quietly.

"Can you see him, dear?" she asked me rather nicely.

"No," I said. "But I know he is here."

"Thank you," she said to me.

"Thank you, Sister," she said to Grandma. "Lyle wants me to try on the shoes, now."

Grandma told her that if she wanted to get more rations, she should see someone in the office. If she wanted some elk meat, she should check with one of the teepees. And then we left.

Outside, Grandma said to me, "I want to thank thee, Rufus. Thee really understands. That helped Dora a lot."

"Grandma," I said, "before we go, I want to do one thing."

"Okay, Rufus," said Grandma. "What is that?"

"I want to see the buffalo," I said. "Are they here in the winter?"

"Rufus," said Grandma sadly, "I'm afraid there are no more buffalo. They were just kidding thee. They have all disappeared. The dung is dried from the droppings of many other animals."

"Where have they gone?" I asked, amazed.

"They were shot by greedy settlers long ago," Grandma said. She sighed, then added, "Well, we have to go see what Joe knows."

George called out to Grandma, "Joe is in the last teepee, waiting to talk with you."

When we went in, Joe was sitting with one woman by the fire; she motioned to us right away. We went and sat down near him and the woman, who was older. Joe was rocking and smoking on a pipe that had some feathers hanging from it. He put the pipe down and said, "We called along the way that they were to go. We learned a little." Then he was quiet some more.

Then Joe said, "My visions tell me that if you leave South Dakota and take the shortest way through Wyoming, like you are going to Little Big Horn where Yellow Hair was defeated, you will come by the place where 'Sunshine' was found in her cradleboard. It was here that a scout, returning this way, found her. And it is near there that she and her family have found refuge for the winter. They have a house near an overhang, overlooking a valley. You will meet them at a place where supplies are sold, just before you come to a town called Colony. They are expecting you in two days."

"Thee has talked to them?" Grandma asked.

"No, I only made two calls," Joe said. "But someone has, or anyway they know you are coming."

The old woman spoke, "He knows these things. And it makes sense, anyway."

"That's right," said Grandma. "Thank thee, Joe. Thank thee, Friend."

We started to get up, and Joe asked, "What do you call your grandson?"

"Rufus," Grandma replied.

"Rufus," Joe said, "do you ride your own horse?"

"No," I said, "but Grandpa let me sit on the plow horse last spring."

"Oh, I see," said Joe. "As soon as you are tall enough to ride, you must learn to ride your own horse."

I looked at Grandma, who nodded and nudged me. "I will," I said, looking at Grandma and wondering if we would have a farm.

As we were leaving, Grandma said to me, "This is important. What he was really trying to tell you, Rufus, was to always think for yourself. But I think learning to ride a horse is a good idea too."

"Won't we be living in a city?" I asked.

"There are a lot of farms around there, don't worry," Grandma said with a smile.

George Pote was coming out of the larger teepee with a group of Sioux men, and they seemed to be having a discussion about something serious. He said to Grandma, "These men are trying to tell me they are not allowed to have rifles to hunt for game on their own land. Is that true?"

Grandma looked worried. "I don't know, George. I wouldn't want to start something at this level. Right now, there is hunger, and what they need most is food. Besides," she said with a laugh, "I thought thee was a vegetarian."

George narrowed his eyes and said, "I am. But they are not. First, they want to turn them in to white men, but if I want to get them hunting licenses so they can hunt like whites, then all of a sudden, they are Indians. Huh?"

"Well, I think for now thee will need to hunt for them," said Grandma firmly. "I think that to fight for their right to hunt is something that needs to come from them, for them. I would be glad to do the research when the time comes. First thing is to head off starvation. Also, I think when their young men return from the war, there will be a greater voice here."

I had never heard Grandma sound so bossy. (Later I learned that my grandmother was an expert on the law and treaties with native tribes, and that helped me to understand why she felt she could do this.)

George Pote looked down at his feet and said, "Sorry, Liz; I'm just frustrated that these people have to live like this. They are grown men and women, and they shouldn't have these stupid rules that make it so hard for them to take care of their families."

"Agreed," said Grandma. "I'm sure the law is on their side. But the law has to be applied, and that is the hard part."

"Okay," George said." I have a little food gathering to do. I will meet you back at the clinic later today."

"Rufus, Barclay, and I will have to leave early tomorrow. We have to be in Wyoming by Monday," said Grandma.

We drove right through Murdo. The roads were pretty clear, and it didn't snow anymore that day. When we got back to the clinic, Grandma said we should make some dinner for George and then get packed for our trip. I helped her cut vegetables, and we made a stew.

It was dark when George got home. He said that he and his friends had not found anything when they went hunting for the tribe. They were going to go the next day and buy some bulk food. After dinner, I took a bath and settled down on the sofa. George and Grandma went over the map again and talked about the way we would travel to get to Wyoming. George thought he knew exactly where Joe meant we should meet Sunshine's family.

George told Grandma he didn't think we needed two days to get to Colony, but Grandma said she wanted to be sure we were there, even if it meant being early.

She said we would stay in a place called Rapid City. We would start out early in the morning from there, just to be sure.

As it turned out, it was a good thing too.

I woke early the next morning because Grandma was making coffee on George's stove and Barclay was thumping across the floor with his cast.

"Grandma," I said, "I think it's First Day. Are we going to Meeting?"

"Thee has been keeping track better than I, Rufus," she answered. "I don't think there is a Meeting close by, and we have to be on the road soon."

"Have we ever missed Meeting before?" I asked.

"Oh, sure," said Grandma, "many times."

"Okay," I said.

George Pote came out in his bathrobe.

"Oh, I need to tell you, you should make sure Barclay gets out and moves around every few hours. His muscles may freeze up and he will get stiff. If you can't get him out, have Rufus get him up on the seat and move his legs for him.

"If you also rub his belly, he won't mind a bit," George added with a smile.

Then he said, "When you get to Washington, you will need to find a doc for Barclay. That cast should come off in about six weeks. They can do an X-ray to see if it has healed right. Also, if he is going to be in the city, you will all be happier if you get him fixed. He won't be running off, then."

THE RIGHT SIDE OF TOWN

We were in the car and headed south, toward Murdo, just as it was beginning to get light. Grandma said that Rapid City was west from there over some winding roads, and she hoped the weather stayed good so the roads would stay open. Right about then it started snowing. The farther west we drove, the harder it snowed.

It seems that the map that George Pote had drawn out took us through the Badlands, which were pretty well closed down. So we had to change our route a little. As we went along, we stopped in small towns at stores and even police stations, and learned a blizzard was due later that afternoon. People were really nice and called ahead for us. They even had us check in at the next town so they could keep track of us if anything happened. Some people thought Grandma was strange in her old-fashioned clothing, and asked questions. One man wanted to know why I wasn't in school.

We seemed to be keeping just ahead of the storm, almost the whole way across South Dakota.

After a while, I asked Grandma if she thought Sunshine would know we were coming.

"I'm almost sure of it," she said.

"If it is like this, with the snow and all, how are we going to find her?" I asked.

"She might find us," Grandma said.

"Okay," I said.

We went along for a while, and then it started snowing again. The road began to climb a bit, and we went through some small towns with silos and sheds built close together. The wind was beginning to blow the snow around. I looked at Grandma to see if she looked worried.

"What's troubling thee, Rufus?" asked Grandma.

"Is this going to be a blizzard?" I asked.

"Yes, probably," said Grandma. "But the sign says that Murphy is just ahead. Then I think it is only about fifteen miles to Rapid City, so it should be fine."

"Okay," I said. I didn't think it was okay. I didn't know how far fifteen miles was.

⚜

Very soon the snow got much heavier and the wind much stronger. Grandma was holding on to the wheel with both hands and sitting up straight. We could still see the power poles, and we could see the buildings in what I think was the town of Murphy. It didn't look like anyone lived in Murphy. But right on the other side of that town, a snowplow pulled out on the road right in front of us.

For some reason Grandma relaxed and smiled. We slowed down but that didn't seem to bother her. We followed the snowplow. It seemed to be getting dark when I asked Grandma what time it was.

She said, "It's one in the afternoon. Sometimes it gets dark like this in a storm, but we will be able to see where we are going as long as we can follow this plow."

"Where is he going?" I asked.

"He's probably has to go to the next town before he can stop or turn around," Grandma said.

Not only did we have the plow to follow, but the road was easier to travel on behind him. After a long time, we seemed to have climbed a ways and then began slowly going down. At last, we came to the outskirts of a town.

Grandma read a big sign that said WELCOME TO RAPID CITY. The plow kept right on going until he turned on a street that looked like it had been plowed recently. He honked his horn and waved as we passed by.

By this time, the wind was blowing and howling.

"Is it a blizzard now?" I asked.

"Almost," said Grandma. "Anyway, let's find someplace to stay for the night."

Grandma did the same thing she had done in Sioux Falls—driving up and down the streets, looking for hotels or motor inns (which is what we called motels then). She found one place but told me to wait in the car. When she came out, she said, "That's not a place we want to stay. They suggest we go to the other side of town."

"Where's that?" I asked.

"Well," she said, "we are on the east side, so it must be the west side, unless they are thinking north and south." She laughed. "The main street seems to go east and west."

The street seemed to climb a little. The snow was coming down hard, and the wind blowing more and more. Grandma saw a sign that read VACANCY.

"At this point," she said, "it doesn't matter what side of town we are on."

We both got out and went in.

"We need a room with a bath," said Grandma.

"No problem," said the man. "That blizzard is really coming on fast. I'll help you folks get everything in and get parked."

"We have a dog on the back seat with his leg in a cast," Grandma said.

"My goodness," said the man. "You've really had a time of it. Let's get your friend in here first, then."

I whispered to Grandma, "I think this is the right side of town."

We went back out to the car, and Barclay pulled himself up. When he started to get out, he put his good paw in the deep snow and then pulled it back.

"It's okay, boy," said the man. He picked Barclay up and carried him inside.

He turned to me and said, "You stay right here with your dog, and I'll get your bags and show your grandma where to park."

So I stood there with Barclay, and after a while the man and Grandma came back with our bags.

It seemed to be a small hotel, not like the big one in Sioux Falls.

Grandma went up to the counter and gave him all the information he asked for. He told Grandma his name was Frank Webster.

He said, "We don't have a restaurant here. But my wife and I try to look out for people in weather like this. So you're welcome to join us for some stew at about six, if you would like. I'll come and knock on your door when it is ready."

"Thank thee," said Grandma.

Frank gave Grandma the key and picked up our bags and followed us. Barclay hobbled along, wagging his tail. The room was like the one in Sioux Falls, but not quite as fancy. It had two beds and a sitting room. It had a bathroom with a tub and sink. It had a big radio in one corner. I looked at Grandma and smiled.

"Okay, Rufus, but not too loud," she said. "Thee may not be able to get much in this weather."

She was right, of course. After playing with the dial for quite a while, I heard a crackling voice saying that a blizzard was predicted for all of western South Dakota and Wyoming and to stay off the roads and indoors. So I turned the radio off.

Barclay was asleep by the heater when there was a knock on the door and Frank asked if we were ready for dinner.

His wife Rose and son Ted were sitting at the table when we arrived.

"Come in, sit down," said Rose. She dished bowls of stew from a large pot in the center of the table. "This is Ted. He is in the third grade this year."

"It's good to meet met thee and thy son," said Grandma. "I'm Elizabeth Thomas and this is my grandson, Rufus."

"Like Rufus Jones," said Ted.

Grandma sat up straight, looking really surprised.

"You are Friends, right?" asked Frank, with a smile.

"How did thee know?" said Grandma.

Everyone laughed except Grandma.

"Lucky guess," said Rose.

Grandma smiled. "Thee and thy family are also Friends, I would guess," she said.

"But you're not in jail or in Europe," I blurted out, looking at Frank.

"Rufus!" Grandma scolded.

He laughed. "No, I was in a Conservation Corps camp, but when my wife got polio, they let me come home. We moved out here from Philadelphia right after Teddy was born and bought this place. When the war started, I registered as a conscientious objector, and they sent me to a forest camp not too far from here. When Rose got sick, she couldn't take care of Ted or run the business. We had to close for a while. She was luckier than some, but it left her partially paralyzed. So she uses her wheelchair most of the time."

"I do most of the cleaning and cooking around here now," said Rose. "Frank does the repairs. We keep things running pretty well. We can be pretty busy some times of the year."

"Are there many Friends here? "asked Grandma.

"We don't know of anyone in Rapid City," said Rose.

"As far as I know, the closest Meeting is in Sheridan. But I don't know if it is still active. We are feeling isolated here. We keep up with Friends back east."

"I forget what day it is," I said. "But we were in Pierre on First Day, and Grandma said it was too early to go to Meeting and she didn't know if there was one. We always go to Meeting at home."

"It doesn't have to be Sunday to go to Meeting," said Ted.

"That's right," said Grandma.

"We could have Meeting after dinner," said Ted.

"After the dishes," corrected Frank, "and then only if everyone wants to."

"I would like that," said Grandma. "I think that we should check on Barclay first."

While the family cleared the dishes, we returned to our room and found that Barclay was up and whining. We took him out to the snow, and he made it yellow and wanted to get back in immediately. Then I gave him some water and some of the food that George had sent along for him. By the time Grandma and I had finished using the bathroom, Barclay was asleep in his bed. So we made our way back to Frank and Rose and Ted's apartment.

We gathered in the living room in silence, and it was familiar and pleasant. I don't think we sat there for an entire hour, but that seemed to be okay. Finally, Rose said how grateful she felt that we had come their way and how nice it was to have the company of Friends.

I was feeling pretty tired. Frank said that if we liked we should stop by in the morning, as he was sure there would be a pot of oatmeal and some coffee for us before we set out, if we set out. The wind was still howling around outside. Both he and Grandma had been talking about how surprised they were that the lights were still on.

Before we went back to our room, he gave us a hurricane lamp, which is just a candle with a glass cover to keep it from blowing out, and some matches.

Our room was at the other end of the hall from their apartment. As we were walking down the hall, I heard a pop, and the lights did go off. Then we heard Barclay barking.

Grandma said, "Wait a minute, Rufus. I'm going to hand thee the lantern and then light a match."

I felt her handing me the lantern and put my hands around the bottom. She lit the match and took the glass off the candle. She quickly lit the candle, put the glass over it, and handed it back to me.

"Looks like we have a dog that is afraid of the dark," said Grandma. "Guess who gets to sleep with him?"

"My guess is, me," I said.

Barclay had tried to get up and get out the door, and he'd fallen down, of course. He was lying there by the door, whining, when we opened it.

"I think we can just sleep in our long underwear tonight," said Grandma.

There was a knock on the door, and when Grandma opened it, Frank was standing there with a flashlight. "We wondered if you were all right. Here is an extra flashlight. Anything I can do?"

Grandma said, "Could thee carry Barclay in and put him on the foot of one of the beds? I'm afraid he has a fear of the dark and none of us will get any sleep unless we baby him."

"Of course," said Frank. "Perhaps we should put a towel down." He carried Barclay in and spent some time talking softly to him.

"If he needs to go, I have a pile of sawdust in the basement, Frank said. "See me in the morning. The snow is pretty deep out there. I'm pretty sure the roads will be closed. Well, good night. Take care."

"Thank thee," said Grandma.

I pulled off my pants, shoes, and sweater and climbed into the bed where Barclay was lying. He had stopped whining. He wiggled his way up closer to me. Before Grandma had put out the candle, he was asleep.

She put the flashlight on the nightstand and said, "If thee has to get up, the flashlight is right here. Don't try to light the candle."

☙

It was daylight, sort of, when Barclay got off the bed with a thud and a yelp. I think he was surprised. He had never slept on a bed before. Grandma was awake but still in bed.

"Go look out the window," she said to me.

I got up and walked across the room to the window. When I pulled the drape aside, the window was completely covered with snow. It wasn't iced over; it was covered with piled-up snow to the top of the window! I pulled the cord so the drapes were wide open and said,

"Grandma, look!"

"Mother of God," said Grandma.

"Um?" I started to ask.

"It's just something I say sometimes," Grandma said. "I don't think we will find Sunshine today."

"Okay," I said. "How do we know how late or early it is?"

"Well," said Grandma, looking at the clock on the nightstand, "the windup clock says almost ten. I think we slept in a bit."

I pulled on my trousers and sweater. Barclay was by the door whining. "I think I better find out where that sawdust is in the basement."

"Thee should ask Frank to show thee," Grandma said.

"Okay," I said.

But I met Ted in the hall, and he took us down the stairs to the basement. We had to carry Barclay.

We brought Barclay back to the room, and Ted said, "Do you want to go up to the second floor and see how high the snow is?"

"Yes!" I said.

We looked out the window at the top of the stairway, and the snow seemed to be just above the first-floor windows.

"Mother of God," I said.

Ted looked at me, shocked. "Are you supposed to say that?"

"I don't know," I said. "It's just something my grandmother says sometimes."

"I never heard that before," Ted said. "Does God even have a mother?"

"I don't know," I said. "I keep asking, but I haven't gotten an answer yet."

I came to learn that many Quakers back then wouldn't have approved of my grandmother's phrase. It was one of the things that she did that made her unique. She was pretty old-fashioned, and then sometimes she just did stuff that was just, well *Grandma.*

"What happens when the snow gets this high?" I asked. "How does the snowplow get out to plow it?"

"All I know is, there is no school," said Ted.

We spent the next two days in Rapid City with Ted and his family. Grandma worried if she would be able to find her friend. Even I told her that if she couldn't go anywhere, probably Sunshine wouldn't be able to go anywhere either. We got to know the Webster family well, and they became friends as well as Friends. Ted helped me with my reading, and I learned how to play chess, sort of. Barclay got stronger and stopped whining about the dark.

No more snow fell, but a big wind did come and blew the snow away some. They got the roads cleared. Finally, on Third Day, December 4, we headed west again.

I was kind of sad to leave my new friend, although we promised to send each other letters. We never did figure out who God's mother was. Ted said that I probably shouldn't repeat it; he thought it was probably only for adults to say.

HORSES APPEAR

$\mathcal{R}$ose packed sandwiches for us. We got Barclay settled in his bed on the floor in the back and said goodbye. As we drove down the street, which was also the highway out of town, it looked like someone had dumped dirt on the road. Grandma said that was for traction, so our tires wouldn't slide all over the place.

We were going to a place called Sturgis, where we could get gas and maybe call ahead to Bellingham and check on things. After that there wouldn't be much until we got to where we were going, and that wasn't much either. That's how Grandma put it to me. She didn't sound really sure about anything. That really didn't worry me; I was beginning to think she could do anything, in her own way, of course.

Sturgis wasn't much of a town. We did get gas, and Grandma called and found out that Thomas B had made it to Bellingham and was waiting in the house for me to get there. That made me feel much better. Boy, did I have some things to tell him.

When we left Sturgis, we drove along twisty roads and up and down a lot. Some of the roads had only been plowed in one lane, so Grandma would honk her horn, because we couldn't always see ahead very far. Once we had to back up for quite a while before we could pull over and let the other car by. But mostly we didn't meet anyone for hours. Finally, we saw a sign that said WELCOME TO WYOMING.

"We are there!" I said excitedly.

"Not quite," said Grandma. "We have some miles to go, and the hard part is that the place is *before* we come to Colony. I hope we don't miss it. And I hope if we come to Colony, we know it. That way at least we can turn around and go back."

"Oh," I said.

After a while we started to slowly climb, and the snow was coming down harder again. Finally, it got darker and we really couldn't see much. It did feel like we were still on the road. I could hear the chains. Grandma slowed down. The wind was whistling, and I thought I heard a clumping kind of sound. Then it felt like we were going down slowly. Suddenly the snow cleared, and on either side of us were people riding horses.

"Mother of God," Grandma said.

A tall man guided his horse in front of the car and seemed to be leading us. So Grandma followed. Soon we were next to an unpainted building with a shed attached to it. The snow here was pretty deep, but it looked like some of it had blown away in places. In other places it piled high against the fences.

"Hello, Grandmother," said the man on the horse when my grandma got out of the car.

Grandma nodded to him.

We all went into the shed, where the horses were tied up and covered with blankets. Then we started in the back door of the store. Barclay was walking beside me, his cast bumping on the rough wood floor.

"The mutt stays in the barn," said the man behind the counter.

"But . . . ," I started to say.

When the smallest horse rider came through the door, a sudden quiet fell on the room. "The dog stays with his family," said a soft dry voice from within the wraps and blankets.

The man behind the counter moved away from it and began working on putting cans on a shelf. Along the walls and in rows out from the walls, large sacks made of coarse material were stacked about six to ten high. There were barrels and bins filled with the kinds of things that were sold in stores in Iowa: pickles, crackers, dry beans, hard candy. But the big feed sacks of burlap were all over the outside wall. Many more than I had seen before. They were filled with oats and dried corn, barley, and even alfalfa for cattle and horses to help them get through the winter when the ground was completely covered with snow and there was nothing to graze on. Pots and pans and washtubs hung from the ceiling. Behind the counter were rifles and boxes of shells. Shovels, picks, and rolls of rope were stacked beside the counter. A potbellied woodstove stood in the center of the front part of the store.

Grandma went over to the woman who had spoken and said, "How is thee, old friend?"

"You already know that," said the woman as she unwound the scarf and blanket, she was wrapped in. "You are late!"

"Well, so is thee," said Grandma.

"I have been here all along," said the woman. "How can I be late?"

"I was snowed in at Rapid City," said Grandma.

"I figured as much," said the woman, who I thought must be Sunshine. "So what now?"

To me, Sunshine was awesome. She was small, just a little bigger than Ted, who was nine years old. Yet she seemed to be the oldest person I had ever seen. Her hair was almost white— maybe silver. Her skin was a very finely wrinkled and a kind of a brownish-red color. It was smooth and soft between the fine lines. I had seen wrinkled skin like this on old Iowa farmers who had spent years in the sun. The color of her skin was beautiful.

There was something else I couldn't describe that made me just stand and stare and then look down whenever I remembered that it wasn't polite to stare. I didn't know what to call it then. Now that I am grown, I know that people say she had a "'presence." I think the closest I could have come up with is that she made you feel calm and respectful at the same time.

When she finally looked at me, she said, "You're Rufus, huh?"

"Yes!" I answered.

"So, I brought you something; something I made for you." She reached inside her shawl and brought out a small bag that had a leather drawstring. It had blue beads sewn into it.

"Thank you," I said, feeling the softness with both hands.

"It's a tobacco pouch," she said, "but I don't want you smoking anything but a peace pipe. Instead you are to put seashells in it when you get to where the Lummi people are."

"Okay," I said. Now I had more to things I had to do: learn to ride a horse and collect seashells.

༃

We were all still standing almost in the doorway, and Barclay was smelling the feed sacks. He looked like he was going to lift a leg when one of the men looked at me and called Barclay out to the shed. The dog didn't hesitate and did what he needed to do.

"So," Sunshine said, turning back to Grandma. "Now what?"

"Well, of course, I wanted to see thee. How does thee think I found thee, old woman?"

"We both know it was Joe!" she answered. "And that answers the next part of my question."

"As always," said Grandma, "thee means more than thee says, and thee believes I am up to more than I am."

"I will find my people and learn my truth," said Sunshine in a very determined voice.

"How could anyone doubt thee?" said Grandma. It wasn't really a question.

"So?" said Sunshine.

The tall man, who had been listening closely, let out a long breath and shook his head. "I am Sam, Sunshine's son," he said, nodding to Grandma.

Grandma smiled and nodded back. "We met before, when you were a boy, I think," she said.

"*So*," said Grandma with emphasis, "just why does thee think thee does not have to take care of thyself while thee does this?"

"Little Girl," said Sunshine, "I have never been a fool. I can die trying to find the truth, or I can die having this fire cut out of me."

I had never heard anyone call my grandmother a little girl before.

I guess when Sunshine first knew her, she was a little girl. It was hard to imagine either of them being little girls, except they were kind of acting like children. They were kind of playing.

"I think," said Grandma, "that now thee is acting like that little boy who did the ghost dance and nearly fell off the cliff, not the respected elder I visited a few years back at Pine Ridge. Why is thee in such a hurry to die, already?"

Sunshine sat down heavily on a feed sack. I think Grandma had won the argument.

"Well," she said, "I don't have much of a plan."

GOOD TALK AND
SLEEPING ON FEED SACKS

"Maybe," said Grandma, taking off her coat and motioning to me to do the same, "thee could introduce thy family, and we could have some coffee and talk a bit."

Grandma paid for cups of coffee, and the man behind the counter poured it into mugs. They all looked a little different from each other. Some of them were chipped.

"This is my son; they call him Sam. And this is my grandson; they call him Little Sam. We got a house up on the ridge," said Sunshine. "I don't know how it all happened, except when we got here, Lois—that's Little Sam's wife—wasn't feeling too good. So we stopped at this place, and that guy, George Wilson"—she nodded at the storekeeper—"says the rancher who owns this part of the state is looking for a caretaker, someone to keep an eye on his cattle and kill coyotes trying to get his cows. So Sam says, 'Okay, we can do that.' So here we are."

"So, what is wrong with Lois?" asked Grandma.

"She's pregnant," said Sam.

"How long will you be here?" asked Grandma, looking at Sunshine.

"They have to stay until spring," said Sunshine. "And I can't get there without them. I am an old woman."

"Right," said Grandma. "And my Aunt Martha is President."

"You don't expect me to ride a horse all the way to Washington in this weather," said Sunshine.

Grandma gave her that smile.

It was quiet for a few minutes.

"So," Grandma said, "Joe says thee has a fire in thy breast, and thee believes him. What does thee think that means?"

"It means," said Sunshine, "that I have cancer and I am going to die."

"Thee might have cancer," said Grandma, "and we are all going to die sometime. Thee may live for a long time. And thee already knows that they can operate on that kind of cancer."

I looked out the window behind where Sam was sitting on a stool. It was snowing fast and hard. The wind was blowing the snow around like it had in Rapid City. I could not even see the road or the other side of the shed that was a few feet from the window. Our car was almost buried.

"Look!" I said, forgetting that I was interrupting.

"Mother of G—" Grandma started to say.

"Oh, yes," said little Sam. "I better call Lois to see that she is all right and let her know we may not get up there tonight."

"Thee has a phone?" Grandma asked, sounding surprised.

"Yes," said Sunshine. "So we can give reports to the rancher."

"How come Joe didn't tell me this?" she asked.

"Because he doesn't know it," said Sunshine.

"So what are we going to do now?" I asked.

"Relax and not worry about it," said Little Sam.

I looked at Grandma. She didn't seem concerned. I looked around the room. There were no beds, and it didn't look like there were any other rooms. If they weren't going home, we probably wouldn't be going anywhere either. I had the feeling that I was just supposed to wait and see what would happen.

"This gives us more than enough time to talk," said Grandma, looking at Sunshine.

"Mother has been stubborn about this," said Sam. "She won't see a doctor, and she won't talk to a healer either."

"I know what's wrong with me!" Sunshine exclaimed. "I don't need some doctor telling me when I'm gonna die!"

"Well, now that we have that settled," said Grandma. Then she started to say something else, but I guess she changed her mind.

"Look, thee can't get away with that with me," Grandma finally said. "I know when someone is aware of their own death, and that is not what thee is talking about. Thee is just being difficult because thee is afraid. Thee is afraid that thee won't be in charge anymore."

"Yes," said Sunshine, softly.

"My friend is a doctor with the Public Health Service in Miles City," Grandma explained.

"He travels around in Montana and the Dakotas. He is not a specialist. He can see thee and tell thee what thee has, maybe. He can refer thee to a specialist."

"Right now," said Sunshine, softly, "the most important thing, for me, is to find my first people."

"I know," said Grandma, "and they are probably in Washington State. There is a good public health hospital in Seattle."

"This is a lot to think about," said Sunshine. "How am I to get to Seattle or Colville or even Miles City?"

It was more like a call for all of us to think, because it was followed by a long silence. It was almost like Meeting, except that the Sioux people sometimes made little noises like they were actually thinking.

"Hmm?" said Sam, looking at Sunshine; and then he looked down at his feet and got quiet.

Sunshine heaved a sigh.

I think Quakers do that too, sometimes. They just keep it to themselves more.

It was very quiet for some time. The only one not thinking was the storekeeper, who was still busy putting things on the shelf. Barclay was asleep by the stove.

After a while, I had an idea. It suddenly came to me how Sunshine could get to Washington. I didn't think I was supposed to talk, because I was a kid. But after I waited for a while, I just couldn't wait anymore. I felt like I had to talk or I would explode or something, so I said very softly, "She could take the train to Washington."

Everyone stirred a little, like they were waking up. They stayed quiet for maybe another minute, and then Sunshine said, "I need a ticket to take the train, dear."

Grandma said, "I know where and how to get a ticket."

The storekeeper, who we thought was paying no attention, said, "I'm a ticket agent."

Sam said, "That white man would sell you a dead horse."

I said, "That's terrible!" looking at the storekeeper and moving a little closer to Grandma.

"Don't worry, son," said Sam. "That's just an Indian joke, like 'He could sell refrigerators to Eskimos.' You know that one?"

"Yeah, I've heard that," I said.

So it seemed to me that it was settled that Sunshine would take the train to Washington, where she could find out about her mother's people. But all was not settled.

"Now, about this friend of yours," said Sunshine, "who you want me to see in Miles City. What is he going to tell me that I don't already know?"

"So," said Grandma, "Joe says that thee has a fire in thy breast. Thee thinks thee has cancer, thee really doesn't know exactly what that means, and thee doesn't want to find out. Why?"

"I don't want anyone cutting into me before I find out what I've come to find out," Sunshine said. "Besides, I'm an old woman; what's the difference?"

"Bull . . . Buffalo chips," said Grandma. Everyone laughed and looked at me.

"Is this thy first great-grandchild?" asked Grandma. "When is the baby due?"

"Yes," said Sam. "About April."

"So when does this job end and what are thy plans?" asked Grandma, looking at Little Sam.

"We will leave when the snow breaks and go where Grandmother is for a while. But we are Sioux and want to return to our people. So after that, we will see," Little Sam answered.

"It seems that this journey that thee is taking," Grandma said to Sunshine, "is not only about thee. It touches many lives. Thee has some responsibilities. Now I think that thee is old enough to know this. Long ago, when my father asked thee what thee would do if there were no wars to be fought, thee told him that the Spirit would show the way. Thee has come a long way, and thee has brought many people with thee. What thee does now is important to those people. So thee has to think of them as well as of thyself.

"Thee has played the games," Grandma went on, "of the little boy and of the old woman with me here. We both know thee is the wise elder and the grandmother. Now thee must decide what thee will do, and what thy family will live with."

And when Grandma finished speaking, we all fell silent again. This time I could tell that it was not that we were helping her think. We were waiting for Sunshine to make up her mind; she seemed to sink deep within herself. It was very quiet. We could hear Barclay snore.

When Sunshine finally spoke, it was dark outside. She said softly, "I will see your friend in Miles City. After that I will take the train to Colville and talk with whoever is left there who may know something. And then we will do what we must. Will you help me with this, Liz?"

Grandma said simply, "Yes."

Sam sighed with relief.

There was no more argument. There was no more discussion about it, then.

That night, we sat around the woodstove and ate things from bags that Grandma bought from the storekeeper. He went to bed in his room after a while.

We sat up and listened to stories that Grandma, Sunshine, and Sam told. Some of the stories were definitely true, some I wasn't sure about, and some I was kind of certain never happened. As we sat there, I looked at all the faces in the firelight and felt that I would always remember that night, even though I was only small. It seemed very special to me. Also, I thought that even adults could work through things if they were honest with themselves.

As the night went on, people found feed sacks, lay down on them, and covered up with a blanket. After a while, I did the same.

I guess feed sacks make a special kind of mattress. I woke up curled up in a hollow place in the middle of the top of the sacks. I think the adults had a harder time, because they were mostly rubbing their backs and stretching. Grandma and Sunshine were sitting by the stove talking.

Grandma got up and got a cup. She poured something from the coffeepot on the stove. "Hey!" she said. "This is just hot water."

"Yeah," said Sunshine. "The seat in the outhouse is a piece of ice."

Grandma groaned. "Will thee go thaw it, so I can make some coffee?" she said, handing her the coffeepot full of hot water.

When Sunshine left, Grandma asked the storekeeper for some change because she had to make phone calls.

"Where are you calling?" He asked.

"Miles City and then Washington State," Grandma answered.

"You're going to need a lot of change," said the storekeeper. "I'll get a roll of quarters and a roll of dimes from the safe, and when you are done, we'll settle the difference."

Sunshine came back with the empty coffeepot, and Grandma fixed the coffee and put the pot on the stove.

"I'll try to reach my friend in Miles City before he starts work. I hope he is not on the road right now."

Grandma got the change and picked up the receiver. The storekeeper said, "Takes a dime to get the operator."

Grandma put a dime in the phone, and it made a clattering sound. "Could I have the operator in Miles City, Montana, please? . . . Okay, just a minute."

She took some quarters and some dimes out and started putting them in the slot in the phone. They made clattering sounds as they fell into the phone. Then she said, "Butte? Could I have Miles City, please? How much?" And she put some more quarters in the phone. More clattering sounds. This was getting entertaining.

"Hello, is this the Miles City operator? Good," said Grandma. "Could I have the home of Walter Marshall? What? Dr. Walter Marshall. Yes, his home. . . . Hello, Meg," said Grandma. "It's Liz Thomas. How is thee? Well, I hope. We are well, although Charles, James, and his wife are in Europe with AFSC just now.

"Actually, Rufus and I are just a short distance away, here in Wyoming. Yes, well. Yes, we would love that. Actually, I was hoping to speak to Bud for just a moment. Is he at home? Oh, really. Thee does? Is thee sure it would be all right?"

Then Grandma listened for a while. "Okay," she said. "And we will have a friend with us. Someone that I was hoping Bud could consult with. She is a native woman, so it is part of his job anyway.

"That's wonderful. Well, probably this afternoon or evening. Can thee give me thy address?"

She put the phone back and turned to us and said, "Well, Walter is away, but he will be back tomorrow and we can stay at his home until then."

"Coffee is ready now," said Sunshine. We had some cookies, and Grandma bought some milk and poured a cup for me. She sent the rest home with Little Sam. Little Sam and Sam went back home to check on Lois and get the things that Sunshine would need for her trip.

"And Sam," she said, "don't forget to bring the cradleboard; there maybe someone there who will recognize it."

Sam smiled.

After breakfast, Grandma went back to the phone. She said, "Operator, Colville Indian agency."

After a long wait, "Well, how about town of Colville? . . . No? Okay, then Spokane. . . . How much?" She put more quarters and dimes in the phone. "Hello, Spokane operator? I am trying to reach the Colville Indian tribe. . . . Okay.

". . . Hello, Spokane Indians? I am trying to reach the Colville Indians. Oh . . . Okay . . . What? Omak. I can remember that. I'll try that. Thank thee." Grandma hung up. She sighed. She looked at the roll of quarters.

"Sunshine," said Grandma, "I don't know if I have enough quarters left to call. Could we try from my friend's house in Miles City? I think it might be easier too."

Sunshine laughed. "Giving birth would be easier!"

Grandma took what was left of the quarters and dimes back to the storekeeper and he counted them. "Twenty-two dollars," he said.

"It's cheaper to just go there," said Grandma.

Sam came back with Sunshine's extra clothes and the cradle-board. It was carefully wrapped in some special cloth. Sunshine showed us what it looked like. It was beautiful. The back board was painted with blue and red patterns that were bright and I had not seen before. There was a tiny little sleeping bag attached with a hood and some straps. I thought it would be pretty hard to climb out.

Grandma packed it carefully in the back of the trunk.

Grandma and I took Barclay for a short walk and he did some business. We talked a bit about horses and learning to ride one. I had been thinking about that. They still seemed pretty tall to me.

I also asked Grandma a question that had bothered me for a while. "Why doesn't Sunshine ride with us? Why is she taking the train?"

"For some reason, probably her illness, she has to use the bathroom very often, and we will be traveling through areas where there is nowhere to stop for many miles," Grandma replied. "Please don't say anything; she is embarrassed."

Sam and Sunshine talked privately for a long time. Then Sam said goodbye, and we three got in the car, ready to head to Miles City.

Grandma insisted that we stop in the town of Colony and eat a real breakfast. She said all the stuff we had been eating at the store wasn't very healthy food. I thought it was kind of fun for a change.

CHIEF JOSEPH

(Washington State Historical Museum)
Hin-mah-too-yah-lat-kekt (Chief Joseph) with his family.
"I hope that no more groans of wounded men and
women will ever go to the ear of the Great Spirit Chief
above, and that all people may be one people."

It was 150 miles to Miles City, and it was a really interesting trip because Sunshine had some amazing things to tell us.

"Grandma," I said. "Today is Third day and it is Twelfth month. What day of the month is it?"

"What?!" said Sunshine, puzzled.

"Rufus," said Grandma, "it's the forth. In other words, it's Tuesday, December fourth. We are really going to have to work hard on this before we get to Washington."

For some reason, probably because there was so much that came into my head at once, I had one of those talking attacks.

"Grandma started to teach me the days of the week, for the real world," I said. "Just then we ran into a snowbank instead of the river. That was before we stayed with George Pote and went to Rosebud and met Dora, whose husband was dead. Nobody could see him but her. She didn't have any shoes or anything to eat. After we found out from Joe where you were, we went to Rapid City and stayed with Ted's family and the lights went out, but that was okay because they were Friends and really nice. Oh, yeah, and George found an elk that was hit by a truck for the people to eat. But Ted and I never figured out if God has a mother, so we gave up on that. And—"

"Rufus, stop!" Grandma exclaimed. "Thee is starting not to make sense."

"But I forgot," I said, "the part about my birthday being on the seventh day of twelfth month."

"Well, yes!" said Grandma, "but I didn't."

"Wild horses running away with that child," said Sunshine.

"Every now and then," said Grandma, "he does get carried away."

"Did he say something about old Dora at Rosebud?" asked Sunshine.

"Yes," said Grandma. "She is having a hard time. Talks to her husband, who died a while back. That's not the only thing; she sees other things, like a line of people waiting for rations. And she is keeping away from everyone. Maybe she is getting senile."

"She goes off like that," Sunshine explained, "when she hasn't eaten for a while."

I said, "I think her husband really is there."

"Yeah," said Sunshine, "he'll move on when he knows she's all right.

"She was a very important part of that group," Sunshine went on. "She always took care of people when they needed something. She was kind of sly in getting around the agents and nuns and getting things for the kids especially. Know how old she is?"

"About eighty?" Grandma guessed.

"Almost one hundred," she replied. "She remembers when no one spoke English and we traded freely."

"I wonder if she got any wood for her stove," I said. "Everyone said they wouldn't get any more until New Year's, whatever that means."

"She'll be all right, Rufus," said Grandma. "People will look out for her."

"As long as she has enough to eat, her thinking is a lot better," said Sunshine. "It's like that for a lot of our older people."

☙

"This place we are going to," said Sunshine, "was named for the white man who killed all those Indians up here: General Miles. Well, I don't know if he was a general or just what. White people named a lot of their places after people like that."

"Who did he kill?" I asked

"A lot of Chief Joseph's people," Sunshine said, "to start with. Joseph and the Nez Perce fought the white soldiers all over Oregon, Idaho, and Montana for months and almost made it to Sitting Bull's camp in Canada."

"They had a war," I said, "right here in America? Why?"

"The white people," said Sunshine, "wanted all the Indians' land. And they kept making promises and then breaking them."

"You mean lying?" I said.

"Right," said Sunshine. "Well, Joseph didn't want to live on a reservation, and he didn't want to be told he had to live like white people."

"Like in a cold house," I said, "instead of a warm teepee."

"But he also didn't want to have a war," said Sunshine. "He had a new baby, and he just wanted to go to the prairie and live a normal life and be left alone. And the government soldiers said they would let him travel and not bother him. He and most of his people traveled over some really rough country, but things stayed peaceful until they camped at a place call Big Hole. It was there that General Gibbon's soldiers attacked, even killing women and children. After that, Joseph's people felt they had to fight."

"Was Chief Joseph sad," I asked, "that some of his people got killed?"

"Very much," Sunshine said. "It broke his heart. He really wasn't a warrior. He was a great leader, but he hated war. He hated killing.

"Some of the younger warriors were angry, and they went out and killed innocent white people. Chief Joseph didn't like that and was angry with them. Also, that made some white people think that Indians were just murderers. They didn't know what happened at Big Hole.

"Right before Joseph started his journey, there was an important battle that the Indians won at a place we call Greasy Grass. It is west of here, in Montana. There was a white General, Yellow Hair, who thought he was better than he really was. Several tribes got together and defeated him so badly that every white soldier was killed. The chief who led that battle was Sitting Bull.

"After the battle, Sitting Bull knew that the white army would be looking for him, so he ran away to Canada, a different country, where he thought they couldn't follow him.

"So when Joseph found it harder to go toward the prairie, he decided to go to Canada and join Sitting Bull. He knew he would be welcome. But what happened was that General Miles caught up with him close to Canada, at Bear Paw. After two days of battle, Chief Joseph gave up because his people were cold and hungry. Many of them were sick or had run away. A few of them did make it to Canada."

"Wow," I said. "And when we were in the teepee, Joe said maybe you are part of Chief Joseph's people."

"Well," said Sunshine, "my blood is Nez Perce; I suppose my heart will always be Sioux."

"I was born on a ship in the Great Atlantic Ocean," I said. "My mother is English, and my father is American, I guess. But I haven't figured out what I am, except I am a Quaker, if that's a thing. I don't know."

"Maybe," said Sunshine, "by the time you are grown, you will be able to be whatever you want."

For some reason we all laughed. I think it was kind of a relief, in a way. I did have one more question, though. "Did Chief Joseph's new baby live, or was she killed by the white soldiers?"

"I don't know if the baby was a boy or a girl," said Sunshine. "But the baby didn't die in the fighting; she died of starvation and cold, or sickness."

It was quiet, then, for a long time. I sat in the back with Barclay and thought about the cold and the snow. I wondered about how Joseph felt. I thought about Mum and Dad and the little children they were helping in that place where the war had been, and I thought about Miles Washington and his having to work in the snow with the wind blowing so hard. I could understand why Sarah and Emily's dad was in jail because he didn't want to fight in a war.

Barclay had been sleeping the whole way. We were quiet for a while, and suddenly he barked in his sleep and woke himself up. He sat up and looked at me. He looked kind of surprised to see me there. I think I hadn't been part of his dream. He managed to turn in a circle and lie back down.

After what seemed like a long time—after Grandma drove around and talked to herself quite a bit—we pulled into a big driveway that made kind of a circle. "This is the address," said Grandma.

A plump, red-haired woman came out of the door as we were getting out of the car. "I am so glad thee made it, Elizabeth. I was beginning to worry. And this is Rufus, of course. And thee must be Sunshine." She held out her hand to Sunshine.

"That is what everyone insists on calling me," said Sunshine.

"What would thee like to be called?" asked Meg Marshall.

"Oh, you don't want to know," said Sunshine, "what else they call me!"

We all laughed. But Grandma rolled her eyes at Sunshine.

I RIDE MY OWN HORSE

We went inside, and Meg Marshall showed us to rooms where we would sleep. It was a very big house. Barclay and I had a room of our own.

There were a lot of windows in the Marshalls' house, and I could see the mountains. They were the tallest I had ever seen. Iowa is very flat. Montana has a lot of mountains. The snow was still very deep. Barclay had to be careful not to get his cast wet, so we cleared a little area of snow for him to use outside. I went out and made a snowman while the adults talked. It was nice to get away from all that serious talk for a while.

We had a big chicken dinner and even listened to the radio for a while after dinner.

Then something happened that hadn't happened since we left Iowa. Grandma said, "Rufus, I would like thee to get thy pajamas and take a bath and get ready for bed."

I felt like I was five years old. Of course, I wouldn't be six for three more days, but it felt strange, all of a sudden, to be treated like a child. I went to my room and got my pajamas out of the suitcase. I took Raggedy Andy out and put him on the bed. I went to the bathroom and found the bathtub full of warm water and a fresh towel set out for me. There was a bright-yellow duck floating in the water. I had one just like that back home. That was what saved the night for me. I felt a little better. Up until then, I was feeling pretty lonely. I would be all alone in that big room, without Grandma or Barclay or anything.

After my bath, I put the towel in the hamper, wiped out the tub and put my clothes back in my bedroom. I went back to the room where the adults were. I sat down next to Grandma.

"Well," I said, "I've slept on couches and in motor inns and hotels and on feed sacks. Oh, and in a big feather bed where I got lost. It has been a long time since I went to sleep in a room all by myself, with just my dog. It's kind of scary."

"What?" said Grandma. "I didn't think of that."

"We won't be far away," said Sunshine.

"Leave thy door open," said Grandma. "We will come to bed soon."

There must have been a lot of stars, because it seemed very bright outside the window. I could see those white, snow-covered mountains. I lay awake for what seemed like a long time, feeling all alone. This house was so big, and I couldn't hear the adults talking. Pretty soon, though, I did hear Barclay snoring. And then it was morning.

⚜

It was Barclay who woke me. He was nudging the bed. I thought he must want to go out. I found my boots and coat and took him out to the place we had cleared.

There were rugs on most of the floors, so his cast didn't make a lot of noise. The house was very quiet. No one was up. I sat on the big sofa in the living room and looked out the window at the fields and the mountains. Then we walked into the dining room and looked out the other windows. I looked into the kitchen. It was not like George Pote's kitchen, with things all over the counter and charts all over the walls. It was very neat and organized. Finally, Barclay and I went back to my room.

It seemed like a long time until Sunshine came into my room. "'Lo," she said.

"'Lo," I said. "It's quiet. And it's so . . ."

"Yeah," she said, "I know."

She sat on the bed, and I showed her some of the pictures of Sioux Falls, from the little books that we got at the hotel. And we laughed about some things. There were pictures of Indians with painted faces, riding white ponies with fancy beaded bridles, and cowboys that looked not at all like the one smoking the cigar in the hotel.

"I guess pictures of real Sioux and real cowboys wouldn't make them no money," said Sunshine.

Finally, Grandma and Meg Marshall got up, and we had breakfast.

Grandma said that we would go to get Sunshine's train ticket, and she thought maybe we could check out finding a place where I could ride a horse for my birthday.

I said, "My birthday isn't today."

"I know," said Grandma, "but we need to find one today, so thee can ride tomorrow."

I didn't really want to stay in that big lonely house one more night. It looked like that was the way it was, though.

Grandma was still trying to find out for sure where the Colville tribe was and where she might find the Nez Perce on their reservation. Who was going to greet Sunshine when she arrived there? It kind of seemed like sending her off into the unknown.

Meg Marshall suggested that we wait until Bud got back from Standing Rock where he had been doing a medical clinic. So we went to a horse ranch. Sunshine thought it was kind of a joke, I could tell. But she was very polite.

Grandma explained to the woman what she wanted. She said that tomorrow was my birthday, and I wanted to ride a horse.

The woman said of course that they have a ring where young children can sit on the horses while they are led around. Meg seemed to think that was a fine thing. Grandma smiled. Then we went into the barn to look at the horses. They were wonderful, but big. I got to pet them. I liked the foals the best.

"That one is just my size," I said.

"Oh," said the woman, "they are too young to ride."

"Maybe we will be back tomorrow," said Meg.

As we were leaving, Sunshine said, "This is wrong, this is not for Rufus. He needs to ride a pony! I bet Joe said he should ride his own horse, right?"

Grandma laughed. "That's right."

"Sometimes we would give a young horse to a young person and have them grow together," said Sunshine. "Although, sometimes they are both too spirited."

We went home for lunch, and Meg called a few friends. She found someone who knew about Shetland ponies a few miles from town. They said I could come, but of course, I would have to ride in the barn because it was so cold.

Bud Marshall came just then, and things livened up a bit.

"Liz. Welcome, Friend. And Rufus, good to see you too. You are Sunshine! Honored! Rufus, I understand that you become six soon. How can we help you with that?"

"Well," I said, smiling because I couldn't help it, "I am going to go ride a pony because Joe from Rosebud told me I should learn to ride my own horse, and that should help a lot. And then I guess Sunshine is going to get to go on the train to find her people in Washington, who were Joseph's people, even though the white soldiers killed so many of his children and made him live on a reservation. And then we are going to Bellingham, and maybe pretty soon my mum and dad will come home from Europe and I will get my bear back. And—"

"Rufus!" exclaimed Grandma, "Stop! Thee is doing it again."

When I finally took a breath and stopped talking, I couldn't remember why I started. I felt dizzy and kind of overwhelmed.

"You have a lot inside," said Bud Marshall, "for such a small package. And it all sounds very important. Perhaps we should sit down and start from the beginning. I need to also talk with Sunshine a bit."

By this time Barclay had managed to get up on his legs and was begging for attention from everyone. Bud Marshall reached down and gave him a good rubdown. We all went into the living room and sat on the sofa and chairs. Bud Marshall took a long match out of a jar by the fireplace and lit the fire, which had already been neatly laid.

"I understand you have been unwell?" he said, looking at Sunshine.

"I don't feel sick," said Sunshine, "but I always have pain."

"What do you do for the pain?"

"Sometimes I chant," said Sunshine. "But only when I am alone. And I had some medicine, but I have had none of that in a long time."

"We need to learn a little about what is wrong," Bud Marshall went on.

"I have cancer," said Sunshine.

"Not all tumors are cancer. Not all cancers are the same. Some grow slowly. If we can take a sample of what you have, we may be able to tell what it is that will have to be done."

"What do you mean, done?" asked Sunshine.

"Sometimes, if there is no cancer," said Bud Marshall, "we can just leave it alone, or just remove the part that is causing the pain. Or if it is real bad cancer, we don't make you go through an operation if it won't help anyway."

"Well," said Sunshine, "I've made it clear that I am going to find my mother's people before I have any surgery."

"Yes, I am not suggesting surgery right now," said Bud Marshall. "Right now, I want to examine you and take a sample of the tumor, if it is a tumor. Then we can know what kind of disease you have and let the people in Seattle know, if that is where you decide to go."

"Seattle?" asked Sunshine.

"That's what I would do," said Bud Marshall, "because that is the best place for you. The reservation has nothing, and they will try to pretend that they are not able to treat you or tell you that no treatment exists. That is very wrong. You have a right to treatment, and Seattle has a government hospital and some very good surgeons."

"Okay," said Sunshine, "when do we do this exam?"

"We will go to the hospital here this afternoon," said Bud Marshall. "You do not have to stay there, and Liz can come with you."

"What am I going to do?" I asked.

"I thought maybe you and Meg could go shopping to get a birthday cake," said Bud. "And then maybe come to the hospital and take an X-ray of Barclay's leg."

"Really?" I said. "Okay."

(I don't think that would be allowed these days, but X-rays were a new thing back then, and no one understood that they weren't all that safe. That you shouldn't just do them for fun.)

Meg Marshall was a nurse and Bud Marshall was one of the few doctors in town at the time, so he had a lot of privileges at the small hospital.

༺ཿ༻

Grandma, Sunshine, and Bud Marshall left right away, and I changed my clothes while Meg Marshall cleaned up around the house and Barclay took another nap. Later, we went to a bakery and picked out a cake and watched them decorate it, which turned out to be more fun than I thought.

We went back to the house and woke Barclay up, got him into the car and took him to the hospital. There was a man who ran the X-ray machine.

"Why don't we use the new fluoroscope instead?" he said. "It is easier and more fun anyway."

So Barclay stood in front of this green light, and we could see the bones in his leg. We could see the bumpy places where he broke his leg and how it was kind of a different shade where it was coming together. The X-ray guy said it wasn't quite strong enough yet for him to be without his cast and that we should definitely have a real X-ray in about two more weeks.

When we got home, everyone else was already there. Grandma and Bud Marshall were in the kitchen fixing dinner.

"Where is Sunshine?" I asked. "Is she all right?"

"She is all right," said Grandma. "Bud has given her medication for pain and she is sleeping."

"What did you find out about her sickness?" I asked the doctor.

"I think it is all in one place," said Bud Marshall, "and that is good. But we won't know the results of the tests for a few days because they have to be looked at by people who know what cancer looks like. It's good that she is taking the train. I want her to rest as much as possible for the next few days. She not as strong as she pretends."

"We need to find out when her train leaves, and also where she should go," said Grandma.

"I have been thinking," said Bud Marshall, "that we should try to contact Friends in the area who might be able to help her. From what I could find out, tribal headquarters are in Colville, but different people live spread out all over North Central and Eastern Washington. Because so many different groups were forced together, there is some unfriendliness among them. A rumor says that two old women near Nespelem rode with Chief Joseph and may still remember something. We may find Friends in Spokane or Wenatchee who might be willing to help her."

He started making phone calls, and Grandma and Meg Marshall finished dinner. I showed Grandma the cake and told her about the fluoroscope of Barclay's leg. Then I took Barclay out for a walk.

Bud checked on Sunshine. He said that she didn't want dinner and would rather sleep some more. At dinner he told us that the train came through Miles at eleven at night. He thought that Sunshine should wait until the next night to go.

⁂

"Well, I am going to see that she has a sleeper car," said Grandma, "if at all possible."

"I also found Friends eager to help," Bud Marshall said. "A Friend who teaches at a college in Walla Walla wants to come with one of her students and go with Sunshine to meet with the women who may know something of her story."

"How will they meet?" said Grandma, a little worried.

"They will meet the train in Spokane and then travel together to Colville and on to Nespelem, once they have confirmed that the women are still there. First, I think, they will try to gather some of the Nez Perce people together to meet with Sunshine."

"We need to figure out where she is going to stay and how her expenses will be paid," said Grandma. "I don't want her to get stuck out there and feel alone and abandoned. Her family will not be out there until spring."

"Somehow," Meg Marshall said with a smile, "she has survived all these years without thy constant care."

Grandma gave her a smile.

"You can give her some cash, and Friends will look after her, I am sure," said Bud Marshall.

Sunshine got up for a while after dinner and joined us by the fire. We had my birthday cake, even though it was two days early, and sang "Happy Birthday." Even though I wasn't going to, I cried because I missed my mum and dad.

Grandma said, "I'm sure there will be a card waiting for thee when we get to Washington."

Bud Marshall told Sunshine that he had found out she could have help finding her people, and she was very pleased. I think Grandma was surprised. Maybe Grandma thought Sunshine would want to do it all without any help.

Meg and Bud Marshall said we would all go to the pony farm after breakfast the next day. And I was tired, so I went to bed gladly that night.

The pony farm was a way out of town over some snowy roads. I rode in the jeep with Bud Marshall, and we talked about what Joe had said to me.

"You know, Rufus," Bud Marshall said, "when Joe says, 'You must ride your own horse,' he is talking like a Sioux man. What a Quaker would say is, 'You must learn to speak your own truth.' Does that make sense?"

"I guess," I said. "It's easier to understand about riding horses when you're a kid, maybe."

Bud laughed. "I guess so. What do you think speaking the truth means?"

I thought about the matches. "Don't tell lies?" I said.

"Well, that is certainly important," said Bud. "But even more important is to speak up when you think something is wrong and not just go along with things the way they are."

"I know," I said, getting excited. "Like how my friend Miles Washington can't get the job he's good at because he has dark-brown skin. That is just wrong."

"Yes, that's it exactly!" said Bud. "Is Miles Washington a Negro?"

"A what?" I said. "I don't know; he is very brown and I'm not, and Sunshine is kind of a different color than we all are. And George Pote says it is because our parents and grandparents gave us things that make us different and also the same."

"Heredity," he said. "George is right, of course; that is all it is. Rufus, I think you are already speaking your own truth. Now let's see about riding that horse."

There was the biggest barn that I had ever seen. It was not very high, but it was round and spread out over a large area. The ponies were short and had long hair. I got to sit on the pony and ride around the barn on the track—first, with the teacher walking beside me telling me what to do, and then I rode all by myself.

I really enjoyed doing this, but after a while my legs and bottom got tired and sore. I felt that I knew what it was like to ride a real horse. I was happy about this. But almost as good as this was the talk Bud Marshall and I had had on the way out. It reminded me of what Sunshine had said. I might enjoy the Indian way of doing things, but my heart would always be Quaker.

When we got back to the house, I was still smiling. I went to my room to change, and while I was there, I even told Raggedy Andy all about the morning. It was a pretty good birthday.

At lunch Meg asked me if there was any present, I might want for my birthday. I said, "Do you know if they make brushes for dogs?" I just kept been thinking that if Miles Washington had a real dog brush he could brush and clean dogs to make some money, and this might make him happy. I thought about that a lot.

Grandma laughed.

"I think they do, Rufus," said Bud Marshall. "I don't know where to find one; maybe in a farm catalog."

"Okay," I said.

"I will look for one and send it on to you." He smiled.

Grandma had been to the train depot, and she had Sunshine's ticket. She gave it to her in an envelope with some money. We were going to have the Marshals take Sunshine to the train. We had to leave so we would get to Spokane in time to meet her train.

"Get a sleeper!" Grandma said firmly. "They told me they had one on that train. Don't let them tell thee any different. Rufus and I have a journey ahead of us," she added.

"Maybe we will see thee at Yearly Meeting," said Meg Marshall as she helped us load the car. I waved to Bud as we pulled out of the driveway.

I had a lot to think about as we drove west from Miles City. I guess I was quiet for a long time.

I must have been in a kind of daydream because when Grandma pointed out the window, I was looking at the bottom of the highest mountains I had ever seen. I had to tilt my head and look up. They were all around.

"Those are mountains," said Grandma, "not hills."

I still didn't say anything for a long time. I was busy looking everywhere. It was a clear day, so we could see all the way to the top of the peaks most of the time.

Grandma finally said, "There are not so many roads in Montana, so it will take us a long time to get across the state. We have to go from east to west but also to the northern part and cross Idaho into Washington. Also, the cities are far apart. So we have to be careful to have a place to stay. The next city is Billings. I don't know exactly when we will get there and what time it will be. After that we have Livingston and that is not so big, so we might have to stay in Billings just to be safe, so thee sees how this goes."

I laughed, and then sighed. "More adventures, I guess."

We rode along a while longer, and then I said, "Grandma, I think grown-ups and kids must think differently."

"Why does thee think that?"

"Well, grown-ups seem to think about big problems sometimes, like how to help everyone. Kids just try to help the people they know. And grown-ups talk about things a lot and how hard they are. And kids do stuff and don't talk so much. But I really don't know very many kids, so I guess I'm not sure. I lot of times, I don't understand grown-ups."

"I think," said Grandma, "that a lot of what happens in the world doesn't make sense, because the people in the world haven't learned to get along very well yet. But also, it is hard for thee to understand how mixed-up and complicated some things are, because there are a lot of things that thee just doesn't know yet."

"Like heredity?" I said.

"Well, that's science," Grandma said. "That might be the easy part. I think the way people act might be harder to understand."

"I learned about what it means 'To ride your own horse' from Bud Marshall," I said. "He said if you're Sioux, like Joe, it makes sense the way he said it. But then he explained that if you're Quaker, it might mean 'To speak your own truth,' and he helped me understand that. I thought about how I felt it was wrong that Miles Washington couldn't get a better job because he has darker skin. And saying that is 'speaking my own truth.' That's the same as riding my own horse. Bud Marshall says that's what Quakers do. I felt good about that."

Grandma smiled. "Yes, standing up for your friends is what Quakers do."

"I want to get Miles Washington a good dog brush," I said, "so he can brush dogs to make money and be happier."

"That's very nice, Rufus," said Grandma. "That is just one thing that we know would make Miles happy. There are many other things, I am sure, that we do not know yet about Miles Washington." She smiled at me.

After a while, Grandma said, "I've been thinking that next summer when thy mum is home, we should come back this way and visit the people we have met and see how they are doing. What do you think?"

"Oh, yes!" I said, "I would really like that."

FIRE AND ROBBERS

Soon after that, we came to Billings. In some ways this was the most unusual place we had stayed. The hotel was pretty new. The room had two comfortable beds. Everything was clean and easy to find. Grandma and I found a place for dinner right next door. I was able to order turkey with cranberry sauce and dressing, and it was almost my birthday. We went to bed early, because Grandma said we were going to drive all the way to Missoula the next day. She said it was the longest drive of all.

Sure enough, we got up before daylight, had coffee and a roll, and were headed west again as the sun was coming up. It did start to snow some, but it had stopped by the time we got to a town called Livingston. We found a place there to eat breakfast.

The people in the restaurant were very friendly. It seemed to make Grandma a little nervous. Some of them stared at her.

A man in one of those big hats, like the man in Sioux Falls, said, "Why aren't you in school, young man?" He wasn't smiling.

"We are moving," said Grandma.

The waitress smiled and asked, "Where are you folks headed to today?"

"Missoula, I hope," Grandma replied.

"It's a ways," said the waitress. "But you should be all right if the weather is good."

After we ate, we stopped for gas and headed right out again. We were really getting high in the mountains again, and Grandma had to slow up a little. We went through a city, Bozeman, which was a little bigger than the last one, but it was only about noon, so Grandma said we were making good time and she was really sure we wouldn't have to stop in Butte.

It wasn't too long until we came to Butte. It was really high in the mountains, and they were close around it. It was a real Old West town. I really wanted to stop and look around. Grandma really didn't want to. And guess what? We didn't stop.

Shortly after we went through Butte, we were both getting hungry. So we stopped in a very small town at a café that had chili. It was good, with lots of beans.

Grandma said, "Now be careful, Rufus, it might be spicy. Drink water."

She was right. I drank a lot of water and milk. I also ate almost the whole bowl of chili.

We headed on through the mountains and snow toward Missoula. There were a lot of tall trees and very few towns now. It was snowing steadily, and it seemed like the trip was taking forever. I wondered if we would get to Washington way ahead of Sunshine.

"No," Grandma said. "Her train can go faster and will go straight to Spokane with no stops."

At one point there was a break in the trees, and we could see that we had come up from a valley and were very high up above a river. At other places we could see the mountains going straight up above us.

There were some carved signs by the road, and Grandma said that we were in a national park. She said that a national park can be very big, much bigger than a city park.

My stomach started to hurt, and I thought about the chili. "Grandma," I said. "I have to use the bathroom."

"Okay," she said. "I'll pull over and you just open the door and stand out in the snow. There is no one around."

"No, Grandma," I said. "Not that kind. My tummy hurts."

"Oh, dear," she said. "It looks like there may be a campground ahead. They may have an outhouse."

She pulled the car off on a plowed road that headed uphill. In a short distance, there were a couple of picnic areas and an outhouse. By one of the picnic areas, two men were huddled around a fire.

"Hmm," said Grandma. "Must be hunters."

I hurried into the outhouse and found a catalog nailed to the wall, just like at the Nelson's.

Just as I was getting up, I heard a loud voice. "I'll be needing some money, ma'am!"

"The gun isn't necessary, Friend. If thee is in need, I am glad to help thee."

"That's a pretty nice car you have there, now isn't it?" said the man loudly. "Me and my brother have someplace we need to get to."

"Thee could hurt someone with that thing. Why doesn't thee just set it down, and we can talk," Grandma pleaded.

I realized one of the men was trying to rob us, and he didn't know I was there. I had an idea. I didn't think too carefully about it. I grabbed the catalog and the matches that were still in my pocket. I lit the catalog and as I left the outhouse. I threw it in the dry winter grass right along the side of the building.

Then I yelled, "Grandma! Fire!"

She reached into the open car door, grabbed a blanket, and threw it to the man, yelling, "Smother the fire! Quick!"

"Rufus," yelled Grandma. "I'll move the car. Grab the shovel!"

The robber was totally confused. He tried to run away.

Almost immediately we heard sirens. A green forest service truck, a sheriff's car, and finally a hose truck arrived. The fire was quickly put out. The sheriff questioned the two men.

"They tried to rob my grandma!" I called out.

Grandma said, "It wouldn't have been a problem, except that he wouldn't put that stupid gun down."

One of the forestry men looked at Grandma and asked, "Are you a Friend?"

"Yes, I am," said Grandma.

"We are COs, waiting for our release date." They were working as conscientious objectors on a national forest project. They were like Ted's father; they didn't believe in war, so they chose to work on a government project instead.

The sheriff was placing the two men in handcuffs and putting them in his car. I had never seen anyone in handcuffs before. It looked kind of uncomfortable.

The sheriff came over and told us that they were wanted already because they had robbed a store and shot the store owner. The store owner was in the hospital but was going to be all right.

Then one of the forest workers came down from where they'd put out the fire with part of the burned catalog in his hand.

"I think someone lit this fire on purpose," he said.

"Why would they do that?" asked the sheriff, looking toward his car.

I was feeling like it was important to tell the truth. But I knew I would be in trouble about the matches.

"I know how it started," I said.

Grandma looked at me, and then I could tell she knew too. Nobody said anything for a few minutes.

"I think thee should tell us about it," said Grandma.

"Okay," I said, taking a deep breath. "Well, you see, we stopped at Mack's Chili shack . . ."

"No, Rufus, "Grandma interrupted. "Just about the fire."

"Oh. Well, I was in the outhouse," I explained, "and I heard this man trying to rob Grandma. So I wanted him to stop, and I am just a kid. So I figured if I started a fire, maybe he would forget about robbing Grandma and try to get away from the fire and we could get away too."

"But what about burning the whole forest down?" asked Grandma.

"I thought the snow would stop it," I said.

"It's against the law to start forest fires on purpose," said the sheriff. "It's against the law to rob nice ladies at gunpoint, also. It is not against the law to try to save your grandmother from a robber. So I have a problem. I guess I can't arrest you. You weren't actually trying to set the forest on fire."

"But you did do one very foolish thing today," continued the sheriff.

"What did I do?" I asked, feeling scared.

"You ate at Mack's Chili Shack," said the sheriff.

The guys from the national forest campground wanted us to stay for dinner, but Grandma said it was important to get on to Missoula. She said she thought we both needed to rest after this experience. The sheriff wrote down what I said about the guy trying to rob Grandma, and had Grandma sign it. We said goodbye to everyone.

When we got back in the car, Grandma said she thought I should put the matches back in the emergency kit, and I did.

All of a sudden, I realized how right Grandma had been. I was really, really tired.

"Boy!" I said, "I feel really, really tired. Like I am really going to sleep and won't even be able to walk to the bed."

"I know," said Grandma. "That happens after something scary or exciting. First, thee gets all the energy thee needs to take care of it, and thee gets excited, and then, when it's over, thee gets really tired."

"Will you be able to drive us all the way to that town?" I asked, yawning.

"It's not very far," said Grandma. "But I think we should get something to eat."

"Not chili!" I said.

Grandma laughed. "The best thing would be breakfast, if we can find a place that will fix it for us."

I thought that was funny, because it was almost dark, but also it sounded just right.

We got to Missoula sooner than I thought we would. Grandma found a café that looked pretty new. When the waitress came, she asked her about breakfast.

While we waited, I asked Grandma, "Why did that man want your car? He had a truck."

"Well, I suppose the car is worth more money," said Grandma. "But in a way, it almost seemed like he enjoyed being mean to people."

"I heard his voice," I said, "and it did sound mean. That's when I thought he was trying to do something bad and not just asking for help."

"Wasn't thee frightened, Rufus?" asked Grandma.

"Well," I said, "I knew I was too little to do anything much, so I had to trick them. I figured that he didn't know I was there. So I decided to start a fire and scare him away. And you were really smart to throw the blanket at him . . . Hey! We didn't get our blanket back!"

"That was pretty brave, Rufus," said Grandma. "Don't worry, we will get another blanket."

🐾

We ate our breakfast-for-dinner and talked about what happened and how we felt. We talked about it like it was happening all over. We talked about the sheriff and the forestry guys. We talked about how fortunate it was that we were so close to their camp. It helped a lot to talk about it.

I felt a little stronger, but I also felt sleepy.

After we paid for our meal, Grandma asked the waitress about a place to stay and got directions to a hotel. They were good directions, because very soon Grandma, Barclay, and I were all in our beds, sleeping.

THE CHRISTMAS PAGEANT

The next morning, I woke up because the sun was shining through the slats in the blinds. Barclay was at the door, looking back at me.

I took Barclay out, and but even the cold air didn't really wake me up. When I got back up to the room, Grandma let me back in, and I gave her the key back.

"Maybe we should sleep late today," I said.

"I'm sure tired," Grandma said. "We have to check out by twelve. I'll set the alarm to eleven."

Even Barclay went right back to sleep. The alarm was one of the big wind-up kinds with the bells on both sides. When it rang, it scared me.

I jumped out of bed and said, "What!?"

I looked around. I wasn't sure where I was. It seemed like it was all part of a dream. I felt tired all over.

"Let's stay over," said Grandma, "and maybe find something to do tonight."

Grandma called down to the office and told them we wanted to stay another night. Then she said we should both take baths and put on clean clothes and look for a place to eat.

When we got down to the lobby, she asked the lady at the desk if she knew of anything fun for a grandmother and a boy to do.

"Why don't you come to the Christmas pageant at my son's school tonight? It should be fun, and we will have refreshments afterward."

"Okay," said Grandma. "Thank thee, that does sound like fun."

"What's a Christmas pageant?" I asked as we walked down the street looking for a place to eat.

"It's a program that the children at the school put on to celebrate Christmas. There will probably be singing and costumes and maybe a story."

"I remember that you and Mum had kind of an argument about Christmas last year. I thought you didn't like to make a big deal about it."

"Rufus," said Grandma, "I've decided that thy mother was right about Christmas. It is a time to celebrate, especially for children. We need to be happy more."

We had breakfast again. Grandma thought maybe after Mack's Chili Shack, breakfast would still be a good idea. On the way back, we crossed the street because Grandma had noticed a dry goods store. She asked if they had a good wool blanket, and then she asked if they might have a small horse brush.

"Yes, we do," said the shopkeeper.

"Does thee think it would be suitable for a long-haired dog?" asked Grandma. "Yes," said the gentleman, "but I use a wide bristle brush on my dog, and it works just fine—just the kind I use for myself."

"Can we see one?"

He reached in back of the counter and brought out a wooden-handled brush that was a little stiff looking. "It'll save you some money," he said, "and my dog likes it just fine."

Grandma said, "Okay. We'll try that."

When we left the store, I reminded Grandma that Bud Marshall was going to send me a real dog brush for Miles Washington. She said, "I know. I was thinking of Barclay."

I thought about what Grandma said about Miles Washington having a lot of other things that made him happy. I wondered how I would know about that. And I thought about how happy Barclay was too.

When we got back to the hotel, Grandma called Bud Marshall and found out that Sunshine had gotten on the train and he had made sure she got her sleeper. The conductor tried to give her a hard time—said they didn't have any left—but Meg Marshall went on the train and found out they did. Grandma said she thought it was because Sunshine is an Indian. I said I thought that was really stupid. Grandma just nodded.

Then she decided to call George Pote to see how things were going. He said he and his friends were able to get more food for the people at Rosebud. That Dora was doing better and was staying in the teepee more.

Grandma told him we might come to visit next summer, and he said, "Good."

The school we went to was a little like Grandpa's college, except the ceilings were much higher. There were a lot of class-rooms with blackboards and small desks all in rows. I had never been in a regular school before. We went into a big room with a stage. We sat on some folding chairs. It seemed like there were parents and grandparents who had come to see the children do the pageant. Grandma said we should sit on an aisle so that I could see, because I might not be able to see over adults in front of me.

After a long wait the lights got dimmer, a curtain on the stage opened, and a girl about Sarah Nelson's age came on stage and said something about shepherds and started to tell a story. As she told the story, children were acting it out on the stage. It was a story about Jesus getting born. I don't think I had heard the story before, although it was something Mum had said before, just not the whole story. I liked the play. The costumes were nice and it was interesting. I wondered what Grandma and I would do if *we* couldn't get a room someday.

After the play some of the older students came on stage and sang songs, and people in the chairs sang too. I didn't know any of the words, but I liked the songs. Then we had cookies and juice. Then they said Santa Claus was coming.

I looked at Grandma. She said, "That's who thy mum calls 'Father Christmas.'"

A man in a red-and-white costume with a white beard came in the door. He gave each of the children a candy cane, said, "Ho, ho, ho," and then went out the door. I had to laugh.

As we walked to the car, Grandma asked, "Well, what did thee think of that?"

"I thought it was funny, and interesting."

(We hadn't ever really celebrated Christmas the way most people do now. Quakers didn't celebrate it back then as much as most do these days. And Santa Claus really wasn't a part of it for little Quaker kids, like he is for some now. However, Christmas was a much bigger deal in Mum's family in England. So she and Grandma had a dispute about this. I guess Grandma was starting to think maybe she liked it better now.)

"I think I will save my candy cane for Mum, though," I said.

The next morning as we were leaving, the lady at the front desk asked how I liked the Christmas pageant, and I told her I thought it was fun.

"And what is Santa going to bring you this year for Christmas?" she asked me.

"I guess," I said, "another candy cane."

She looked confused. "Well, have a nice trip," she said.

As we loaded the car and helped Barclay get settled, I realized that I didn't know where we were going next. Grandma got behind the wheel and looked at a piece of paper she had written some notes on during her talk on the phone.

"Well, it's over the mountains and through Idaho to Washington today," she said.

"Will we get all the way there today?" I asked.

"To Washington State," she said. "But not to Bellingham. We have to meet Sunshine and give her the cradleboard. We have to find out what her plans are and where she is going to be."

"Where are we going next?" I asked.

"Spokane," she said, "then we will call Bud and see if Sunshine or the Friends have checked in with him yet. Then we will know what to do."

"So are we going to stay in Spokane and go to another pageant," I said, and then laughed so she would know I was kidding.

"Oh, I think thee has gone to one, that will do," Grandma replied.

"Lookout Pass is high," Grandma said as we started to climb, "and the roads may have fresh snow. I hope the weather is good. They talked of more snow on the radio this morning, so don't be surprised if it is very heavy in the mountains."

"So we are going to be in Washington State today," I said, "and that is where we are going to live."

"Thee may be surprised," said Grandma, "because the part of Washington State we are in today will be very different from the part we are going to live in."

"Really?" I said. "What do you mean?"

"Spokane will seem a lot like Montana, maybe a little flatter. There will be snow and it will still be cold, probably. There is a river, with buildings along it, like the towns we saw in South Dakota and Montana. When we get to the other part of Washington there probably won't be snow. Thee will see part of the Pacific Ocean, and maybe it will be raining. It will be warmer. It will not seem like winter to thee."

"That *is* different," I said.

I thought about that. I didn't remember seeing the ocean. I was only a few days old when we were on the Atlantic Ocean. So I had never really seen the ocean. That was exciting. I thought about that a lot as we traveled through the mountains. It was a winding road, and the snow was heavy and there was wind, but not a blizzard.

Barclay was a little restless. Grandma thought he might be cold. She asked me to put the new blanket over him. That seemed to settle him down for a while.

We finally got to Lookout Pass. Grandma said we were in Idaho. She said that the part of Idaho we were going through was very skinny and it would take about one hour. We started going downhill on a windy road, past farms and trees and lakes. The trees were green and tall. Only a few trees had bare branches like in Iowa. There were cows and pigs and sheep, though. I started to see places where they kept grain, and mills where they cut logs. It was looking a lot like the towns I was used to.

Then Grandma said we were in Washington. That seemed really exciting to me. At last we had gotten to the place where we were going, sort of. We had come a long way. It wasn't very late, though.

"There is a hotel we will stay at here, Rufus," said Grandma. "I will call Bud, and then we will meet with some Friends who have invited us to dinner."

"I didn't know," I said, "that we knew anyone here."

"We don't yet," she said. "By Friends, I mean Quakers."

"Okay," I said.

When she called, Bud told Grandma that he had not heard yet from Sunshine, but he thought she might call later. He said the people helping her might be able to meet us at a place called

Wenatchee, which wasn't too far from where they were. Grandma agreed to call him back that night.

We went to a house, which was up on a hill not too far from downtown, and met a lot of people from the local Meeting. It was First Day. I had forgotten the days with all the things we had been doing! There were children there as well as adults of all ages. We had a good time. For some reason, a lot of these Quakers had red hair. Grandma said that she thought they were probably part of the same family.

We stayed for a long time. When we got back to the hotel room, Grandma called Bud, who said that Sunshine and the women she was with had called him. They wanted to meet in Wenatchee the next day at about two in the afternoon. He gave her an address and some directions. He also told her that he got the results from the Sunshine's medical tests. She did have cancer. He said he still felt that she had enough time before she had to have surgery, so she could have it in a few months when her family could come. And he said something to Grandma about working to make sure she would get to have the operation in Seattle. I didn't understand, at the time, but it was something Grandma especially had to work on.

SUNSHINE'S PEOPLE

*G*randma wanted to get going early, and again, she forgot about breakfast.

"Grandma," I said, "I'm hungry."

She stopped at a bakery and got two rolls and two coffees. Lucky for me she got lots of cream and sugar.

The trip over the roads this time looked a lot like Iowa except for the rolling hills. There were silos and fields, with barns and cows in fenced lots. The roads were dotted with little town and stores. After a couple of hours, we came to a huge cement waterfall. Grandma explained that it was a dam. It had been built only a few years before to make electricity from the river's rapid water, and to use some of the water to irrigate the crops. She said that stopping the river did cause some problems. It flooded some land, and it made it impossible for the fish to swim upstream to lay their eggs and have babies. Then she surprised me by saying, "So that's the job thy father will have when he comes home: making fish ladders."

"What?" I said. "Ladders for fish? If Barclay can't climb a ladder, how can a fish?"

"Well," Grandma said, "it's not exactly that kind of ladder, but it works."

I was willing to believe it, but only if they could explain it. For now, the dam was amazing enough. We left, and we were early enough to find a place for lunch. By the time we got to Wenatchee, we were still early, so we drove around and looked at things.

The place we were going to meet Sunshine and the women she was with was the home of a Quaker family who had an apple farm. When we got there, Sunshine was not there yet. Grandma took the cradleboard out of the trunk of the car. She didn't unwrap it. We went to the door and a woman came to answer.

"You must be Elizabeth and Rufus Thomas. Welcome. Come in! I am Martha Wallace. They called to let me know they are just a little late. Perhaps you would like some tea?"

I noticed Martha was dressed like Grandma. I had not seen that since we left Iowa.

Soon she returned with cups of tea and also some milk and cookies.

"Thank you," I said.

Soon a station wagon pulled into the driveway, and a young woman got out and came to the door. Martha Wallace answered the door and came back to tell us that Sunshine and her friends had arrived. And another car had pulled in right behind their car.

They all came into the living room, and Sunshine gave Grandma a hug.

The Friends nodded to her, and the two elderly native women stood with their arms folded. They were wrapped in blankets. They did not seem friendly to me. Martha Wallace motioned for everyone to have a seat. She had placed several chairs around the room in a circle.

"These women have been trying to help me," Sunshine said. "They wonder if maybe I was the daughter of a woman expecting a child, who left sometime after Deep Hole. Her husband was killed and she just couldn't go on without him, so one day she just disappeared.

"They say that they cannot think of anyone else who could have been in that part of Wyoming or South Dakota about then."

"Many of our people," said one of the women, "were killed by white soldiers at Deep Hole, even women and children who were running away."

"It was not only the Nez Perce," said the other elder. "Many peoples suffered greatly in those times. We do not know who you might be. If we see the cradleboard, we may know if it is one of our tribe's or not."

Grandma handed the bundle to Sunshine, who carefully unwound the cloth that was wrapped around the cradleboard. It was covered in deerskin and delicately embroidered with colored beads.

Both of the elders gasped. One of them said something in her language. They sat there in silence for what seemed like a long time.

"I thought she was killed," said the older of the two. "She was our sister. She ran with her baby, but the soldiers were chasing them. She must have gone a long way."

"This means you . . . you are my sister's daughter, the one that was born on the trail that winter," said the other.

"We were only children then," she said. "We cried, but we had to keep on. Somehow we made it, and our mother too. Finally, we came here with Joseph, and he died. And now we are old. We have found you. We thought you were dead."

They went on talking like this for quite some time. It was getting dark outside. Grandma went into the kitchen, and Martha Wallace followed her. Even though I was very young, I could tell they were very excited. Yet they spoke in a very dignified manner, as though this had become a very important occasion. It was like suddenly they became warm and friendly, but in a way that was very grown up.

Grandma came back and said, "Sunshine, I have to let you know what Bud said about your tests."

So Sunshine followed Grandma out to the kitchen, and they talked for a few minutes. Then they both came in and sat down.

"I have to decide what I should do for the next few months," said Sunshine. "I have cancer and have to have an operation in Seattle this spring. So I can go back to Wyoming and stay with my son and grandson. Or I can stay on the reservation here, as I have my small allotment, maybe. I can go back to Pine Ridge or Standing Rock."

"You're going to come and live with us," said the elders together.

"I have very little," said Sunshine, "to contribute."

"So?" said the older sister. "You can't make us any poorer than we are."

"Okay," said Grandma. "I need to be able to reach you."

The elders gave her an address and the phone number for the agency.

"I think we have to leave soon," said Grandma. "We have several hours to go before we are home."

That sounded so strange to me. I hadn't thought about arriving at my new home that night. I wondered if Thomas B would be waiting for me. I was so used to traveling by now, I wasn't sure that I was ready to be "home" just yet.

We said goodbye. We said we would see Sunshine soon. And as we got back in the car, I remembered that maybe Barclay should get out and walk. Grandma stood by the car while Barclay smelled the snow and did what he did. Then I carefully covered him, and we headed to our new home.

We were driving west through the next town and into the woods when we saw some sawhorses and a sign across the road that Grandma read aloud: PASS CLOSED.

"What does that mean?" I asked.

"It means that we can't drive over the mountain tonight," said Grandma.

"Oh, no!" I laughed "What if there is no room at the inn?"

Grandma turned the car around and headed back to Wenatchee, where we did find room at the inn.

GOD'S MOTHER

I woke up before Grandma the next morning. We were on the third or fourth floor of a hotel, and I could see the river from the window. I could also see some more mountains in the west. I thought we were a lot closer than that to the mountains. It seemed like they had moved away during the night.

Barclay woke, stood up, and shook himself. Then Grandma sat up in bed. I was standing by the window.

"Grandma," I said, "I didn't think the mountains were so far away yesterday. It seems like we have a long way to go."

She came over and looked out the window. "Oh," she said, "those are not the mountains we have to cross. Those are the Olympic Mountains; they are farther still, by the Pacific Ocean."

She pointed to some hills and mountains that were very close. "We are already in the mountains that we have to cross," she said.

❀

We got dressed and went down to the lobby. They had a restaurant there, and we ate breakfast. Grandma asked the lady at the desk how we could find out if the pass was open. She called the state police, then said that they thought it would be open both ways by ten o'clock.

We went back up to our room, and Grandma called her brother. His name was William and he lived in Bellingham too. She talked to him and told him we would be there by afternoon.

"Will there by anyone home?" she said. "I want to get the key and the mail."

"Thee will. Good. We'll be happy to see thee too."

She turned to me.

"Okay, Rufus," said Grandma. "Let's go."

⚜

Barclay got up and headed for the door, and we followed. He seemed just as eager as we were.

Outside it was snowing lightly, and as we loaded things into the car, I thought about how this was the last time I would have to sleep in a hotel for a long time. Tonight, I could sleep in my own bed in my own house. In my mind, I pictured our house in Iowa, only in Bellingham. I sort of knew it would be a different house. I just couldn't imagine anything different.

We went back the way we had come the day before. We passed the farmhouse where Sunshine had learned who her family was and went on to the road where the "Pass Closed" sign had been. This time it was set off to the side of the road instead of blocking it. Grandma read another sign that said, CHAINS REQUIRED. We had our chains on; they had been on since South Dakota.

Right away, we started to go up. We kept going up and around on the curving roads. There was a lot of snow, and some places we had to slow down a lot. When we got to the very top, Grandma read a sign that said, SUMMIT, and then we started going down.

Soon there were a few towns, with restaurants and stores that seemed to sell skis and clothes. Then the snow started to turn to rain and the road got slushy. There was more traffic. I could hear our chains making a clunking noise on the pavement.

Then there was a flashing light behind us, and Grandma said. "Uh-oh," and pulled the car over to the side of the road.

A police car pulled up behind us, and a policeman got out and came to Grandma's window.

"Did you see the 'Chains Off' sign a few miles back?" the officer asked.

"No," said Grandma, "I'm sorry. We have had these on since the garage put them on in South Dakota. I'm not sure how to take them off."

The officer looked at her license and looked at me and Barclay.

"If thee could just allow me," said Grandma, "to get to a garage, I will have them removed."

"I can help you ma'am," said the officer, "if you will set your parking brake."

He did something to each wheel, then he asked Grandma to pull forward a little. He picked up the cables off the side of the road and put them on the floor of the back seat.

He came back to the window, and Grandma said: "Thank thee."

"Are you just visiting Washington? Or going to be living here?" he asked.

"We are moving to Bellingham," Grandma answered. "My husband, my son, and his wife are in Europe, but they will be joining us soon."

"It would be good if you could have someone show you how to put on and take off chains," he advised, "because we do a lot of that up here."

Now as I looked around, it seemed like winter was gone. Only everywhere there were colorful lights along the streets and in people's windows. Some people had green wreaths hanging on their front doors.

Finally, the rain got lighter and stopped. We were no longer going downhill so much. There were many more farms and houses and towns.

"Oh, my," Grandma whispered as she pulled the car off the road. "Look, Rufus! Don't move, just look!"

There, a short way up the road, were a mother bear and two small cubs crossing into the woods. I had never seen a bear before. They didn't look at us but kept moving, the babies following their mother.

"It is very unusual for them to be out of hibernation this time of year," Grandma said. "Probably there was blasting for the dam and they were forced out to find a safer place to finish their winter sleep." She explained that bears hibernate during the winter, and that it is during the winter that their cubs are born.

"So," I said, "it is not a good season for bears to move either!"

After a while Grandma said, "I've been looking at a map and it will take a little longer, but I want to take a highway that will take us by some saltwater views. This saltwater is a kind of finger of the Pacific Ocean called Puget Sound. We will go through some small cities and towns too."

Pretty soon we went over a bridge and several small bridges, and we did see the water, which looked like an ocean to me, except I could see land off in the distance on the other side of the water. Grandma said that it was not China but just more of Washington State, or some islands. There was a lot to look at.

At one place we were so close to the water and by a park that when we got out to walk Barclay, Grandma and I threw a rock in the water.

"Finally," Grandma said as we went drove into a town, "there is the college where thy grandfather is going to teach. And now I just need to figure out where our new house is!"

I was excited, but unfortunately, it took quite a while to find our house. There were streets and avenues with the same names.

Finally, after driving around for a while, Grandma went to the post office and asked there. They gave her very careful directions. Our house was on a hill. But the street was pretty flat. We finally parked in front.

I was surprised because it wasn't very much like our house in Iowa. It was big and tall. It had a big porch that went most of the way around it. There were several steps going up to the porch in front. The front door had a big glass window.

Grandma and I sat looking at the house for a few minutes.

"Is that house just for us?" I asked.

"I think so," said Grandma.

"Well, Rufus," she added after a moment, "why doesn't thee try the door and look around while I go down the street and get the key and mail from Uncle William."

I went up on the porch and looked in the big window on the door. There, sitting on a box on a step of the stairway that went upstairs, was Thomas B!

The door handle was the kind with a lever that you pull down. I reached up and tried to pull it down. I pushed the door. It didn't open. I jiggled the handle and shook the door. I looked at Thomas B again. All of a sudden, he shook and fell off his box right onto the door handle, and it swung open. (To this day I am sure I heard him laughing. Probably it was all some kind of accident. Still, that is how I remember it.)

I sat down on the staircase, right then and there, and tried to tell him everything that I'd been wanting to tell him all these weeks. All our things and boxes were there, and there were a lot! There in a corner was Grandma's chair. It seemed like Grandma did not take long enough to get the keys and mail.

"Sorry I took so long, Rufus," she said. "Thy uncle had so much he needed to tell me. Oh, I see thee has found thy bear. I knew it would be all right."

"Oh, by the way, thee has a letter from George Pote. Would thee like me to read it to thee?"

"Yes!" I said.

Grandma opened the letter and read:

Dear Rufus,

I had to go to Sioux City to get some supplies and decided to look up your friend Miles Washington. We had lunch together, and I was able to give him a grooming brush, which I told him you wanted him to have. He said it will help him earn a little extra, if there are folks who have dogs to groom. We talked for quite a while. It seems that he used to be a jockey. (That's a person who rides racehorses.) But he was hurt in the war. He really would like to be a teacher. He has three children and would like to work with children. He hopes he can go to college someday. He said to tell you hello, and I am enclosing his address so that you can write to him.

Your Friend,
George Pote

"I'm so glad he got a brush," I said. "I want to write him a letter too."

I hugged Thomas B and smiled at Grandma. Everything was all right.

"Would thee mind getting Barclay out of the car," she asked, "and taking him for a walk?"

"Okay," I said.

"I'm going to look over the mail," Grandma said, settling into a chair. "We can bring in our things from the car a little later."

I put Thomas B in a chair by her and said, "Keep an eye on him, okay?"

Barclay had been wondering what was going on. He was sitting up in his bed in the car, whining. I got him out and tied the rope to his collar. We walked down the block along the parking strip.

I was watching Barclay and not paying much attention, when I heard a voice say, "Hey, are you the kid who's moving into the house on the corner?"

"Hello. Yes," I said, looking around. There was a boy, a little smaller, but I thought about my age, with black hair and a baseball cap.

"Do you have," said the boy, who was now standing next to me, "an Uncle William?"

"Yes, I think so," I said. "I just moved from Iowa, so I haven't met him yet."

"I'm Tommy," said the boy. "I moved from Idaho, but I have met your Uncle Will; my Grandpa knows him really well."

"I'm Rufus," I said. "I live with my Grandma. My mum and dad and grandpa are in Europe. But they'll be home soon, and then my grandpa is going to teach, and my dad is going to make ladders for fish, and my mum is going to be a nurse."

"Yeah," said Tommy, "my dad has been in Europe too. When he gets back, he's going to be a farmer."

"Good," I said.

That made a lot more sense to me than building fish ladders.

"I live in that apartment," said Tommy, pointing at a brick building down the street and across a small side street.

Just then a woman called, "Tommy, time for dinner!" And he took off toward the building. I walked back to the house with Barclay.

As we headed into the living room, I saw Grandma sitting in her favorite chair. She had an open letter in her lap. She was crying.

"Great Mother of God," she said. "Help us now!"

"Does G . . . ," I started to say and then stopped myself.

"Yes, Rufus," sobbed Grandma. "Now even God needs a mother to rock Him in Her arms."

My grandmother didn't cry very often. At least, I didn't see her cry very much. I felt kind of confused and a little scared.

"Grandma," I asked, trying not to cry. "What's wrong?"

"Oh, Rufus," she said, pulling me to her and giving me a big hug. "The family is fine. Thy mother is coming home soon. So that's good news. But she is overwhelmed with all the suffering, and she needs to be with thee.

"I am sad because of the terrible things that have happened in this war. Thy mother has written about some of them, and I think these things that happened would make God sad also."

Grandma looked out the window. It was already dark, but I could still see the rain in the streetlight.

"Oh, we are supposed to be at thy uncle's for dinner," she said. "It's a special dinner."

Uncle William lived in the next block. We walked there through the rain. We left Barclay sleeping on the rug in the living room. He already seemed to feel at home.

SHARING MY BIRTHDAY

$\mathcal{U}$ncle William's house had an entry with a lot of hats and coats hanging on the wall, and boots on the floor. It was raining, so there was a lot of water on the floor also. Grandma put our coats on a hook, on top of someone else's coat. She didn't think the floor was a good idea.

"Will! Catherine!" she called. "We're here."

A woman in a faded flowered dress appeared in the archway.

"Hi . . . Rufus?" she said. "I'm Aunt Catherine. Come on in; you're almost late." She led us into a big room with a table and a fireplace.

"Well, hello, Rufus! Did you know that we have the same birthday?" said a man with a white beard.

"This is your Uncle William," said Grandma.

"Hi," I said, smiling.

He looked a bit like Santa, except Uncle William's beard was obviously real. He was sitting at a big table with some young men and women, and some children too. It was a long table, but the chairs were kind of crowded together.

Uncle William introduced me to all my cousins at the table. They were three of his children and some of his grandchildren. All of the kids there were older than me. I paid attention, but I wasn't sure I was going to be able to remember everyone's name.

"Now, come and sit by me," said Uncle William. "We are celebrating your birthday too."

Aunt Catherine, William's wife, brought a huge bowl of spaghetti and meatballs and set it in the center of the table. I wondered how she knew this was my favorite.

Aunt Catherine said, "Let's have some silence."

After silent grace, we were eating and people were talking to each other, so it was kind of noisy. I asked Uncle William about Tommy, the boy I had met that afternoon.

He said he knew Tommy, and he knew Tommy's grandpa really well. They had been best friends for a long time. His name was Robert Hayes, and Uncle William told me a good story about how Tommy's grandparents got married:

"In 1915, there was a big world's fair in San Francisco, and Robert decided to go. One night he was walking along the waterfront when he noticed a young woman in a traditional Japanese kimono who seemed to be about to jump from one of the high piers. He yelled for her to stop and ran out to her.

"She told him that someone had been mean to her and had caused her to be pregnant. Because he wouldn't marry her and she had no husband, she had brought shame to her family and thought she had to die. Robert was so shocked. And also, his heart was moved. So right away he said, 'I will marry you.' They argued a bit, but there was no way that he was he was going to let her jump off the dock. She finally agreed, and he brought her back to Washington, where they were married."

"Did his Meeting agree?" I asked.

Uncle William laughed. He had a wonderful deep laugh that seemed to roll on, like a song.

"Not everyone is a Quaker, Rufus," he said.

Then Aunt Catherine appeared with a cake, and everyone started singing and clapping. There weren't any candles. Someone handed Uncle William a present. He jiggled it and tried guess what was in the package. When he finally opened it, there was a hat in the box. It was a gray hat with a black band. It was not a Quaker hat.

"Well, Rufus," said Grandma. "Thy mother and father have sent thee something." She reached under the table and pulled out a long package wrapped in brown paper.

It seemed very long. I had to stand up to open it. One of the cousins helped me. It was a stick! It was a beautiful stick with little pictures carved into it. I was confused. What would I do with a stick?

"Read the card," said Uncle William.

"'Dear Rufus,'" I read, "'this is an Irish walking stick.'" I paused.

"I am having trouble with the rest."

Uncle William looked over my shoulder and read, "'It is called a shillelagh. We think it will be useful when you go hiking in Washington. We love you. Your Mum will see you soon.'"

I looked at the walking stick and turned it around and around in my hands. My parents had sent it to me, all that way. It was really special.

"Maybe," said Uncle William, "you can use that tomorrow when we go up in the woods to get Christmas trees."

"What?" said Grandma. "We have a lot of unpacking to do, and I have to make plans for Sunshine."

"Relax," said Aunt Catherine. "Tommy's mother, Janet Hayes, and I are going to be lots of help, and first we will all go get those trees." Aunt Catherine was soft-spoken, but remarkably firm. I think Grandma was also tired. She didn't argue.

❧

So that's the way it was. When we got home that night, there were already beds made for us. We got into them and slept; I with my shillelagh, and I bet Grandma slept in her long underwear too. I was looking forward to seeing Mum and to having some fun with my new friend.

But that's another story, for another time.

EPILOGUE

"*So, did you get a tree, Grandpa Rufus? Did you see Tommy again? When did your Mum come home? Did you ever see Miles Washington again?" we asked.*

"*Next time," said Grandpa Rufus. "Now it's time to get into the sleeping bags and get to sleep. Tomorrow I want you all up in time for Meeting.*"

CPSIA information can be obtained
at www.ICGtesting.com
Printed in the USA
FFHW012024191119
56085810-62119FF